FAVAS CAN BE FATAL

A Novel of Suspense

FAVAS CAN BE FATAL

A Novel of Suspense

PRISCILLA ROYAL

alyson books
NEW YORK

Manufactured in the United States of America.

This trade paperback original is published by Alyson Books,
P.O. Box 1253, Old Chelsea Station, New York, New York 10113-1251.
Distribution in the United Kingdom by Turnaround Publisher Services Ltd.,
Unit 3, Olympia Trading Estate, Coburg Road, Wood Green,
London N22 6TZ England.

First edition: April 2006

06 07 08 09 10 **a** 10 9 8 7 6 5 4 3 2 1

ISBN 1-55583-946-0
ISBN-13 978-1-55583-946-8

Library of Congress Cataloging-in-Publication Data has been applied for.

Book design by Taylor Johnson.

To Katherine V. Forrest with gratitude for all you have done to make this possible. Your own books have long been an inspiration; your teaching of the craft is invaluable.

Acknowledgements:

Kris Brandenberger, Bonnie DeClark, Liz Hartka, Henie Lentz,
Anne Maczulak, Monty Montee, Michael Nava, Sheldon Siegel,
Meg Stiefvater, and Janet Wallace

CHAPTER 1

IT WAS HOTTER than a morning in hell the day he died. Of course people die in Livorno, but rarely for suspicious reasons. Crime is a city thing, you know. Violence just doesn't happen in bucolic little seacoast towns—even near San Francisco. And Livorno is definitely bucolic, tacked to the side of the sometimes-green hills of the northern California coast. It was an Italian fishing village at the turn of the twentieth century. The smell of fresh oregano still mixes with the scent of ocean air and not-so-fresh seaweed on warm summer mornings.

The houses in town are a jumble: mini Victorians, unpretentious clapboard cottages, the ubiquitous ranch style, and recently, energy-efficient bi-levels on postage-stamp lots. But every yard has some sort of garden, even the postage stamps. A few are filled with half-wild fuchsias, overblown old roses, or tomatoes mixed in with green and yellow zucchini. There are grapevines here and there and some century-old bougainvillea, hidden behind walls from the fierce coastal winds. Their pink and purple petals drop and drift with impunity across town.

Frances and I moved to Livorno in the '70s. It was her idea. She was a painter and fell in love with the colors and light of the area. I fell in love with her, and I went where she was happy. It was a very easy decision.

Five years ago, on a rainy winter night, Frances came into San Francisco to meet me for dinner after I left work. A DUI truck driver running a red light hit her in a crosswalk. She actually died when he jammed his transmission into reverse and backed over her head. It was his first offense, and, the attorney argued, the guy had clearly tried to stop. He got a suspended sentence. Grief, however, is for life.

After her death, I should have moved, but I stayed in our home, both numbed and comforted by memories and routine. Conventional wisdom said to move back to San Francisco, eliminate an awful commute, and get on with life.

I am not, however, conventional. And there was another reason for staying. A very good one: It was that rare and precious thing called friendship.

LORENZA GALLI IS my neighbor and dearest friend. She also owns The Lovage, a vegetarian restaurant in an eggplant-colored Victorian with green trim, which, unfortunately, is on the main street of Livorno. I say "unfortunately" because it is the most god-awful color combination I have ever seen—a real civic eyesore. Lorenza's response to that comment was to remind me that no one would ever have any trouble finding the place, which makes good business sense if you have out-of-town customers. I suppose she's right. Nonetheless, I still try not to open my eyes until I'm inside.

I provide Lorenza with a few of her fresh vegetables and most of her herbs. She insists on paying me something, so I bill her costs. That makes her feel better. Three or four seed packets with the occasional bag of fertilizer thrown in aren't worth the argument, and I always manage to forget an item here and there, which makes me feel better.

After Frances died, I found some solace in growing things as a hobby. But I couldn't even bear to kill pests eating the plants, so I learned to garden organically: you get slugs drunk with beer and hose aphids off your vegetables onto something else you don't care about. Organics may have been the "in" thing of the '90s. I didn't care much one way or the other about that. Nonlethal gardening was, quite simply, comforting.

Nor did Lorenza start The Lovage out of any desire to be "in" either. She became a vegetarian after her husband, George, dropped dead on their patio five months after his triple bypass surgery. The idea of a restaurant came later as a way to handle her grief and perhaps expiate an unnecessary guilt over George's death. After all, how could anyone have known at that time that so many steaks and gravies could be lethal?

"Because I knew better, Alice, that's why," Lorenza had sputtered at me when she was able to talk about it a bit. "No one in either of our families died in their forties. We ate fresh vegetables from our gardens. And pasta. Lots of fruit. The only fat we had was olive oil. But George didn't want to eat Italian. In those days, you were either foreign or American. We couldn't be hyphenated. So he killed himself trying to be some kind of generic American who doesn't even exist. My father didn't die until he was past ninety and only then because his heart was broken over my mother's death." She sniffed back a tear. "I hate steak."

"What did your mother die of?" I had asked, innocently trying to change the subject. I didn't want Lorenza to start thinking about how often she, personally, might have cooked the perpetrator that she now believed had killed her husband.

"Stroke. She was yelling at Dad because she thought he was flirting with a widow at church Bingo."

"Was he?"

"Probably."

I smiled. After a minute, so did Lorenza.

Actually, it didn't make any difference why Lorenza had decided to open The Lovage. The food was wonderful. It wasn't long before eager eaters were clogging the streets with their cars as they unclogged their arteries with her vegetable ragoûts and pasta primaveras. It was sufficiently successful that Lorenza had just hired a new chef a couple of months ago so she could spend more time on the business, recipes, and menus. It was also so successful that she was about to be reviewed by the food critic diners read as gospel and restaurateurs hated on sight: Arthur Peters.

CHAPTER 2

I DON'T KNOW how the day began for Peters, but, for me, it began with my beloved neighbor hanging over our mutual fence with a scowl on her face.

"Are those damned herbs ready yet?" Lorenza was clearly not in a good mood.

"I'd show you what I've cut, but that look would wilt a rock," I said sweetly. The heat was almost unbearable. Perfect tomato weather. Indeed, my prize Romas were tight to bursting, the onions were so sweet you could die for them, and the smell from my bed of fresh garlic would have raised those who had. I had been up early, before the morning dew was gone, cutting enough lovage, oregano, and basil for an entire Roman army, as I had promised her.

"Think the look will work on Peters?" Lorenza took a deep breath. "I'm sorry, Alice. I didn't mean to snap. I'm just nervous."

I put a dirt-streaked and sweaty hand on her arm. "It's okay. As long as you don't call me 'Alicia,' I'll never take anything you say personally!"

Alicia Susannah McDoughall is my real name. I changed it to Alice and dropped the Susannah when I was four, much to my mother's aggravation. The simplification had nothing to do with rebellion against a certain middle-class fussiness. It had all to do with falling in love with Alice in Wonderland and especially that great Cheshire cat. The war between my mother and me on which name she'll call me has exceeded the forty-year mark and threatens to pass the half century.

"I'm not suicidal; only your mother would dare do that." For just a moment Lorenza's brown eyes twinkled with amusement, then she looked down at my hand and patted it. "I need moral support. I'm scared about tonight. Come down to the restaurant with me?"

"I was hoping you'd ask." (Actually, I had already planned my outfit.) "But you really have nothing to worry about. He's going to die over your artichoke-tomato fettuccine...if he survives the fennel, mushroom, and Parmesan salad. He may just flip his obvious hairpiece."

"One sarcastic review from Peters, and restaurants have been known to close doors almost overnight."

A slight exaggeration, I was about to say. She had certainly built enough of a reputation not to care what Peters wrote. But I decided to shut up. Nerves are normal for any restaurant owner on review night, and, in fact, she did have a valid concern.

Peters had an incredible influence with diners who read his column. I could never understand why people would stop going somewhere they liked just because he panned it. And Peters could be vicious. He always let a place know when he was coming. He said that let a chef show off his best. This was, however, usually less than a blessing to The Reviewed. One chef said he didn't need to salt his food that night because his own nervous sweat added more than enough to the stew. To top it all off for Lorenza, Peters's prior reviews indicated strongly that he believed no woman could manage a good restaurant or cook professionally. If he wrote even a passing review on The Lovage, with both a woman owner and a woman chef, it would be a first.

So I opted for the soothing lie.

"Not to worry! With you at the helm, nothing could possibly go wrong. And, if it does, you can live on the proceeds from your wine cellar until Peters drops dead of excess bile."

I always believe in fallback plans to soothing lies.

BY THE TIME Lorenza came for me, the herbs and vegetables were washed, dried, and ready for delivery. So was I. Edward and Piers, my two precious felines, had dry food in their bowls for whenever they decided it was cool enough to bother with eating. Since it was a special evening, I opted for some beaten bronze earrings from North Africa and a multitextured bead necklace to add to the usual.

At 222 pounds of solid love handle, I had been assigned long ago by the American fashion industry to eternity in a muumuu. Being of British ancestry, however, my DNA has a fair share of that imperial certitude which had once turned much of the world maps pink. After a generation or so in America, that certitude got translated into the cult of the individual. With such a dynamite combo working for me, I looked at what clothing the industry offered, rejected fashion as a plot against female security, and found my clothes in stores catering to cultures that saw no shame in a size 24. I developed an entire wardrobe around flowing skirts of coarse weave and vibrant patterns from South-American Indian styles, short-sleeved cotton pullover blouses from India, and, on those rare occasions when I'm cold, shawls from Mexico. If I didn't work in San Francisco, I would have been fired years ago for my Cost Plus style of dress in a ditto-suited workplace.

In any event, Lorenza actually smiled when she saw me. Either she liked the outfit or she was just happy I hadn't forgotten the herbs.

"YOU HAVEN'T MET Emma yet."

I grunted. Lorenza was driving, and riding with my dear friend down our charming little hairpin turns into the center of town is always an experience guaranteed to remind me of how Moses must have felt whenever he talked to God. I vaguely remembered, through my haze of utter panic, that Emma was the new chef.

"You'll like her."

Actually, I just hoped to survive the next turn without discovering the properties of a car, two passengers, and a couple of boxes of herbs and vegetables suddenly thrust into spontaneous flight.

Of course, we always did survive the entire hill of turns. I had no faith, however, that gravity would not one day meet its match in Lorenza's speed—and I have never enjoyed flying. In any event, I was so busy thanking whatever gods there might be for our safe arrival on the main street that I forgot to shut my eyes against the offensive coloring of the restaurant.

"Cute car," I said, quickly concentrating on the much more pleasant view of a tall and slender woman slipping into a little red Miata, then quickly but expertly pulling away from the curb.

"Why don't you buy one?"

"I don't like convertibles. I just like its shape: round and cute."

"I prefer boxy cars like this one." Lorenza affectionately patted the dashboard of her Sentra.

"Box = coffin" popped into my mind. The image did not bode well for my increased confidence on our next trip down the hill in her car.

But we had gotten there, and Lorenza, as usual, parked behind the restaurant in the garage, which might have comfortably housed one family horse when it was first built at the turn of the century. It did not, however, comfortably house two Sentras, which, although hardly large cars, were pretty snug together. I assumed the other white one belonged to the new chef.

Once at the restaurant, Lorenza is all business. Thus my dear friend, at five foot nine and 140 pounds, completely forgot that some of us don't squeeze through small spaces as well as once we had when we were lithe young women with wasp waists, small breasts, and no stomachs. Long skirt swishing gracefully, she leapt from the car, grabbed a load from the backseat, and rushed from the scene, leaving me with a major puzzle on how to get out.

"Next time, will you please remember that I am a ripe and mature woman, not a wraith like you. I need room to get out of this damned car!" I growled in pointless frustration after the departed Lorenza.

First I tried the door on my side, but the chef's car was too close. I chose to take this personally and muttered something derogatory involving canines. By the time I had hefted feet, legs, hips, and skirts over the automatic transmission, dashboard, and steering wheel, I was sweating, mad, and ready for war. The proverbial straw came when I finally hoisted myself loose of the car and found that Lorenza had taken the light box of herbs, leaving me with the heavier one filled with vegetables in the trunk.

"May the next salad you make have a fly in it, Lorenza!" I muttered at the spare tire.

"Beg pardon?"

I spun around. Standing behind me, dressed in chef's whites, was a slender woman of about my height with thick, natural blond hair brushed back into an eighteenth-century–style queue. She looked at me unwaveringly with large and intelligent hazel eyes from behind small-frame glasses. She had an impressive, thirtysomething, roses-under-cream complexion. Perhaps not a classically beautiful woman, I thought, but she had a magnetic something in the combination of her features. I caught myself staring at her. But reading a barely controlled impatience, perhaps even a bit of contempt in her intense gaze, I suddenly felt foolish and embarrassed and took an instant dislike to her.

"You're Emma?" I said in a firm monotone, trying to regain my self-confidence.

She nodded.

"I'm Alice."

I lifted the box of vegetables from the trunk, dumped it into her arms, and stood silently with hands on hips.

We continued to stare at each other.

Finally getting the hint, she turned and carried the carton back to the restaurant.

I immediately felt much better.

I AM OFTEN amazed at the kind of woman Lorenza thinks I will like. Of course, part of the problem is knowing what she means by *like.* Sometimes she forgets I'm gay; sometimes she remembers.

Sometimes *like* means a potential friend; sometimes it means a date. At one of Lorenza's parties, I remember finding the woman I was supposed to "like" quite interesting and attractive. Luckily, I met the devoted husband before I made a bloody fool of myself. On another occasion, the woman in question would have been great fun at what I call blood-gushing sporting events, crushing beer cans, but I don't like that kind of sport. She didn't like classical music, and neither of us saw enough in the other to bend our respective spines.

And now I had just met Emma, whom I was supposed to "like." Well, I saw no wedding ring on the finger when she reached for the box. However, I don't like blondes (perhaps because my mother pretends to be one), so dating was out of the question, and I don't like being made to feel a fool, so friendship was out too. I just wish Lorenza would quit trying to get me out of my happy little rut and leave me in peace.

I took in a deep lungful of hot air. At least my sweat had dried. Amazing what a good temper tantrum will do. I decided I would feel better if I had a cool glass of my favorite white Burgundy from Lorenza's store and began to trudge up the path toward the back door of The Lovage.

I WAS DEFINITELY out of shape, and the stairs in this heat were more than I could do in one uninterrupted hike. Halfway up, I stopped to catch my breath.

It really was a shame, I thought, that Elena García, Lorenza's sous-chef, had turned down the offer of head chef. At barely five feet tall, she was a veritable cyclone of energy and had worked with Lorenza from the beginning. I liked her peppery view of life, skill with food, and ability to organize. She was like family and had always been a second right hand for Lorenza. But she suffered from severe migraines and decided the extra pressure wasn't worth the probable added pain.

Hence Emma. So now, in addition to a staff still having to adjust to a new person with a different way of doing things, we had Emma, the sixty-day wonder, in charge of the kitchen the night Peters was doing his first review. I wasn't too happy about this. Lorenza, on the other hand, seemed confident about her new chef's skills. Maybe she was just being her usual kind and supportive self.

Whatever. It was time to get over my snit and get on with being the good friend she really needed right now. I began to sigh dramatically, then stopped just in time. Having no desire to choke on my grand gesture, I glanced down at the Dumpster. Thank goodness, the garbage company must have just emptied it. On a day this hot, the stench of rotting vegetables, no matter how organic, would have been toxic.

Having hoisted myself up the last few stairs, I started to open the screen door when I noticed a large earthenware bowl covered in plastic wrap, sitting on a shelf attached to the railing near some pots of edible flowers. I touched it. Luckily it was still cool. Lorenza had probably put it there so she could open the door. It was just like her to put something down and forget about it. And Emma probably didn't see it with the vegetable box in her arms. Well, it wouldn't be the first time I had saved an ingredient for the evening menu. I picked the thing up and walked into the kitchen.

Lorenza, Elena, and Emma were nowhere to be seen. The rest of the staff was busy chopping, shredding, mixing, and whatever. I dropped the bowl next to the box of vegetables from the car. The kitchen was so hot I left the door to the porch open. Surely the screen would keep any insect protein from polluting this vegetarian sanctuary. The place did need air. Emma could shut it herself if she wanted to suffocate.

Then I went to find Lorenza in the dining room.

ONE OF THE reasons I love The Lovage is the dining room. The floor is polished hardwood. The tables are monastic weight, painted a thick flat white and matched to forest green taverna chairs with brown woven seats. In the middle of each table is an earthenware bowl of Native American or African design filled with fresh grapes, small green apples, cherries, tangerines, or whatever took Lorenza's fancy at the market on any given day. The water glasses remind me of old, hand-blown wine bottles, cut off at the curve and smoothed for drinking the chilled bottled waters offered from a list. Bunches of drying herbs hang from the ceiling. The room is fresh, earthy, with a graceful bow to the dreamily peaceful simplicities of other imagined times. This is a place to be at rest and enjoy good food with good company. Would it get through to Peters? From what I'd heard, I doubted it.

As I walked into the dining room, Elena flew past, but not before she gave me a quick but warm hug. Lorenza was standing in a far corner, waving her hands over her servers in what looked like a benediction but was more likely an attempt to describe the specials of the night. Maybe a benediction wouldn't hurt either, I decided, and I'm not religious.

Opting not to interrupt the ceremony, I wandered over to the stack of freshly typed menus to see what delicacies awaited our Peters. I scanned the list quickly, blinked, and scanned again more slowly. Indeed, she had included some good stuff, but this was not the killer list of unique Lovage specialties I had hoped for. Lorenza had been far too conservative in making these particular choices, no matter how well she did them. She had included my favorite fennel, mushroom, and Parmesan salad, but I would have omitted the ubiquitous mixed baby green salad with balsamic vinaigrette for the review night. Everyone does that. Knowing Peters, I guessed he'd pick that just so he could say it was really no different from a hundred like it.

I would also have been happier with one of the many eggplant entrées Lorenza does so well, which, according to a story I once read, would have won her a sultan for a husband in the old days of the Ottoman Empire. With this menu, she might need that sultan after tonight.

Instead she had picked a vegetarian bean burrito, a wild mushroom frittata with mint, and a cliché-sounding spinach lasagna to complete the entrée list. There was no point in perusing the desserts. They couldn't save her. I knew what Peters would pick to hang her on. The burrito. He'd just love comparing it to Taco Bell.

This was definitely not the time to tell Lorenza what I thought of her menu. Maybe it was the time for me to find that glass of white Burgundy I had promised myself. The edges of what would not be a fun evening needed softening.

WINEGLASS IN HAND, I sat outside on the top step of the staircase with a wonderful view of the debris box and ex-horse barn. The kitchen noises behind me were soothingly familiar, and a cool evening breeze was coming up, the natural air conditioning that keeps this town bearable in the summer.

Two sips of my wine, and the edges of many rough evenings were indeed softening. I began to think back on summers with Frances when we would take an hour in evenings like this to sit out back of the house and talk about our respective days. Sometimes we would just hold hands, breathe in the scent of jasmine curling around the posts of the old grape arbor, and dream dreams. Despite the wine, I felt a deep, sharp, and twisting stab of longing.

"Alice? Where are you?"

Since I was about to start crying into my wine, I suppose I should have been grateful to Lorenza for the interruption, but I wasn't. It seemed such a perfect evening for morbid self-pity. On the other hand, it was probably going to be Lorenza's time for morbid self-pity. I could have mine another night. So I shrugged, struggled to my feet, took a final sip of wine, and shouted, "Out here on the terrace!"

Lorenza's normally healthy-looking olive complexion was gray-green. Not a good sign. I put down my wineglass and hugged her.

"He's going to be here any minute." Her voice was harsh with tension.

I looked at my watch and then down the hall toward the dining area. According to his reservation time, Peters would indeed be arriving any second. It was going on six, and I could hear a first-rate din, which signified lots of customers. Normally, that would be a joyous sound, but tonight it made me think all too much of crowd commotion at a medieval execution.

"Give me the seat by the kitchen where I can watch," I said. "If things get too dicey, I'll pretend to choke, and you can save my life. With headlines like 'Restaurateur Saves Customer,' no one will even care about his review." I was trying to make her laugh, but the words all came out sounding rather desperate even to my own ears.

"Don't choke. He'd hold off the review or else blame your choking on my food. Believe me, if we survive tonight, I'm going to light a few candles to the patron saint of restaurants."

Didn't know there was one, I thought, and was about to make some quip when I glanced behind her at Emma. Her complexion now more closely resembled rose with blight. With both of them in a state nearing nervous frenzy, this was clearly not the time for one of my flippant remarks.

"Buy the candles," I said.

I DID GET my usual table by the kitchen entrance. Most customers find such seating unacceptable, but, at The Lovage, it is the best place in the house for people watching. The wall is only big enough for a small, two-person table, but it allows a view of the entire dining room—perfect for tonight.

Lorenza offered me more wine and anything I wanted to eat. I opted for a nicely chilled bottle of Evian water, a little cheese, a little fruit, and waited for the show to begin. It didn't take long.

CHAPTER 3

PETERS WOULD HAVE made either a great politician or a good drag queen. Frances and I had seen him in action a couple of times when we had joined Lorenza and George for dinner at some new place in San Francisco. Unlike most restaurant critics, he is notorious for putting on a show, public reputation being half showmanship of course. And he never comes alone. He has his small entourage, which usually includes the exquisitely dressed and stylishly beautiful girlfriend, the male secretary, and an equally smashing female guest. The girlfriend and secretary have been fixtures for several years now. The female guest was recently added, perhaps in an attempt by his publisher to increase female visibility and thus quash those nasty little Letters to the Editor that suggested Peters was not exactly an equal-opportunity reviewer.

Frances and I used to joke that the girlfriend was actually a robotic Barbie doll and the male secretary an actor hired for a long run. After all, who else could stand him? Of course neither of us was fooled by the insipid ploy to make him look like a man with a gender negative view of women. And we did wonder about the secretary, who was just too handsome to be straight. Whatever the truths, the party was one guaranteed to catch your attention, and that's exactly what he wanted.

And tonight, that's exactly what he got. The otherwise pleasant clatter and chatter of merry feeders came to a halt when the Peters party walked to the center of the dining room. He had specifically reserved that table. I was surprised he hadn't requested that the floor be raised a few inches for dramatic effect. He had asked, however, that the surrounding tables be distanced more than usual from his. The theater had indeed lost a talent when Peters opted for a career in food.

Since I had never been this close to the Peters party before, I amused myself for a few minutes watching as the two men helped the female guests settle themselves into their respective chairs. The women were almost interchangeable: fake blonde, model height, model weight, and good clothes hangers. To be fair, they had gotten themselves up well and perhaps I was just a tad jealous. On the other hand, I was just itching to pinch one of them to see if she had real skin or was a battery-operated mannequin.

Suddenly, as if she had read my rather rude thought, the woman, presumed to be Peters's date, turned around and stared directly at me. I shuddered as if a chill had gone through me. She resembled an eerily resurrected Marilyn Monroe, caught with all her childlike fragility and haunted vulnerability showing. For just a second, we stared at each other, and I felt an almost unbearable intensity of raw emotion flowing from her. Quickly, I looked down at the table.

When I looked back, she had shifted her gaze and was obviously having problems with her contacts. She held a tissue to her eye and was blinking vigorously. Clearly, the wine had gotten to my imagination. Smiling in relief, I decided to muse instead on my fruit and cheese.

But his date was unquestionably an attractive woman of a certain type. I never understood why Peters seemed to appeal to women. Perhaps, as Frances would have said, I'm genetically incapable of appreciating that chemical *je ne sais quoi* men have. On the other hand, I have no problem appreciating gentleness or thoughtfulness in men, neither quality being evident in Peters. To me, at least, he was not good-looking, admittedly an opinion founded in taste and not in fact. He was well over six feet, gangly, horse-faced in a way only a mare could really find beautiful, and balding. The bald part would have been rather endearing had he not chosen to plop the most godawful rug I had ever seen on the otherwise innocuous spot.

Have I given the impression yet that I don't like Peters? Well, let's not be subtle here; I don't. I have read his column for years. He usually writes with entertaining wit and unquestionably finds real joy in the subject of creativity and food. Those are the pluses. The negatives deeply disturb me.

For starters, when he got his divorce many years ago, he used his food column to suggest his soon-to-be-ex-wife was an alcoholic. One of his remarks was something like: "A little more wine in the stew and less in the glass might save a marriage, dear hearts!" Not that he mentioned his ex-wife by name. He didn't need to. We all knew whom he meant, and a drinking problem was not a good thing to suggest about a woman who was a well-known physician in town.

His former wife did file a libel suit, which was dropped after he made a public apology for "any misunderstanding about the impeccable character" of his ex-spouse. Although he carefully avoided overt attacks on women after that, he did start on a major campaign to rid the culinary world of anything "wimpish." Oddly enough, *wimp* did not equal *gay,* and he had never been known to make an antigay remark, nor did he have a pattern of writing negative reviews of openly gay chefs. He just attacked women owners and, even then, saved his greatest venom for those with women as head chefs as well. Some would argue that I should be at least halfway content with a lack of gay bigotry. Not exactly. In my book, intolerance is like crabgrass: one plant and, in short order, the whole yard's infested.

PETERS PUT DOWN his menu. Everything was finally set for the commencement of the feeding ritual. The servers hovered. The two women accepted what they were told they should eat. King Arthur raised his head and pronounced his own choice.

I knew it! The burrito.

I felt sick. I'm not sure whether the taste in my mouth was the bile of broken dreams or the wine, water, fruit, and cheese backing up on me. Whichever, I shoved my plate aside and watched, with an ugly sense of foreboding, the arrival of the mixed baby green salads to the center table.

Peters was in his finest form. He picked up his fork and looked down at the salad with a well-practiced expression of boyish anticipation. Then ever so slowly his eyebrows rose, his eyes grew large, and an expression of perplexed but mildly disappointed surprise flowed across his face. His party, none of whom had yet lifted a fork, watched him in silent concentration, as did most of the other diners—including me.

Was there a worm in the arugula?

After one small bite, he dipped his fingers gingerly into the salad and pulled up a leaf from which flowed a cascade of olive oil. "John! Call my attorney," he said with a good-humored smile to his secretary. "I want mineral rights. I do believe I've struck oil!"

I winced. Lorenza was dead in the water before we even got to Taco Bell.

Lorenza shot to his side like the proverbial bullet, shooing servers away to the safety of other customers. I couldn't hear what she said, but it wasn't important. He waved her words aside with benevolent dismissal.

"Quite all right, dear heart," he said loudly. "I'll skip the salad. Maybe some bread will cut that oily taste in my mouth. I'm sure the main course will be better." His not very subtle version of "honey" and the dismissive pat on her arm made Lorenza draw back. His toothy smile that brought the image of Caligula to mind didn't help instill confidence either.

While Peters continued his one-sided discussion with Lorenza, the rest of his party idly punctured leaves of salad greens with their forks. Only the secretary took a bite, then tilted his head to one side, made a face, and put down his fork. The servers belatedly swarmed and whisked the salads away, unfortunately not into oblivion.

Enter the burrito. Peters knew he was on Easy Street with this one. In fact, he almost looked bored. He didn't even have to break a sweat to do this restaurant in. The staff was doing it for him.

He took his fork and gingerly rolled the burrito over. "A little damp," he announced. "Can't be oil, now can it? Wouldn't be any left in the kitchen after that salad!" The middle-aged couple at a nearby table laughed. He pointed at them, with that all-inclusive gesture old pols use so well, and smiled broadly. Thrilled to be noticed by a local celebrity, the man of the couple puffed his chest out like a pigeon, and the woman giggled girlishly.

Carefully, Peters cut into the burrito and pulled out some of the stuffing. "My goodness! What do we have here? Green pea and library paste? How creative! May not be edible, but it certainly does look, shall we say, unique? Well, we'll all be fair and give it a real taste." And he nodded to the girlfriend who had ordered the same entrée. She raised her fork and joined him in a hefty bite of the stuff.

My temper was close to the flashpoint. Between the salad fiasco and the bizarre burrito filling, which had never been known to grace Lorenza's repertoire before, I was convinced there was something rotten in the kitchen and it was spelled E-M-M-A. I rose from my table, gestured at my stricken friend that I was off to investigate, and sailed like a large destroyer down the hall in search of the so-called chef.

Oddly enough, I saw no chef.

Had Elena not been there to give direction and pitch in with whatever needed doing, there would have been utter chaos in the kitchen. The Lovage had gotten so busy recently that Lorenza desperately needed more employees, but interviews and reference checks took time. And tonight of all nights two of the staff had called in sick. The rest were working feverishly to keep up with the orders of the diners other than Peters. Lorenza was busy trying to placate him and could do nothing to help. And yet Emma, who was supposed to be in charge, was nowhere to be seen. Emma's absence just added to the problem of too few people trying to do too much at one time.

"Thank goodness for Elena!" I muttered and, now like a hunting hound, went off on the scent of the missing cook.

The staff bathroom was empty, as was the storage room and the wine cellar. The only person washing dishes had a nose ring I didn't remember seeing on Emma. As much as I hated to interrupt her, I stopped Elena in mid-chop.

"Where is she?"

"On the back porch. She needed some air, she said." Elena rolled her dark brown eyes skyward, a gesture of annoyance I rarely saw her use.

"She'll need more than air when I get through with her," I said, sucking in a few inches of stomach and easing my way in a crablike fashion through all the commotion.

Swinging open the door and screen, I saw Emma leaning against the back railing, with her face hidden in her hands, sobbing.

"And what in the hell do you think you're doing?" I asked.

Emma never had a chance to answer. Suddenly, from behind me, Lorenza grabbed my arm.

"We've got to call 911," she said hoarsely. "I think Peters just dropped dead."

CHAPTER 4

MEMORY BECOMES SURREAL faced with any death but especially one in such unexpected circumstances as Peters's. Some details of that night I have completely forgotten, yet other things I remember with a clarity way out of proportion or with peculiar intensity.

When I walked back into the dining room, there was utter confusion, of course. I remember one server telling another that he had already tried the Heimlich procedure. Someone else was shouting "Doctor! Doctor!" in a hysterical monotone. I think that was the fellow next to Peters who had been so thrilled with the attention of a famous person. Lorenza and his female companion finally managed to quiet him down.

There must have been a lot of noise, but I only remember the almost palpable sound of communal breathing. Maybe that was when Lorenza walked to the center of the room and quite calmly told everyone to stay where they were, that help and the police were on the way. There must have been silence then.

And I just could not keep my eyes off the corpse. There it was, the former Peters, his face lying square in the middle of the plate, his wig flipped over the water glass, leaving his fading bald spot pitifully naked. It seemed cruel not to put the hairpiece back on his head, but even I knew better. I let it be and tried to stare elsewhere, like at his girlfriend.

She was sitting, hunched over the table, her blonde hair hiding her face, while she slowly and carefully shoved her half-eaten burrito, back and forth, across the plate. I became almost mesmerized by her activity as if it were the most important thing I could ever watch.

Then the woman next to her, the secretary's guest, began to retch. Lorenza put her arm around her and whisked her off to the bathroom. I remember an unearthly wail coming from the rear of the restaurant. I guessed it was the woman. It seemed forever before Lorenza led her back, put her at a table where she couldn't see Peters, and gave her a glass of something amber, probably brandy.

Peters's secretary sat with a blank stare. He had the plastic smile of someone who was told ages ago that his picture was going to be taken at any minute. Then he reached into his jacket, pulled out a cigarette, and lit it. The Lovage is nonsmoking; no one said a word.

The police did come quickly, Lorenza told me later. I don't recall much about any of that. She said they had spread out, asking customers and staff what had happened. I do recollect one officer asking Peters's secretary about next of kin and something about medical history. He finally stopped smiling, which is the only reason that sticks in my mind.

But I certainly remember the officer in charge. Thompson was her name. She was squat, a little stocky, in slacks and a sports jacket. Brown hair so short it looked spiky. Really butch. I doubt those legs had seen a skirt since she moved away from maternal oversight. I found myself wondering if she ever bothered to shave them. Definitely not my usual type.

Nonetheless, I did catch myself thinking she was rather cute. She had a smile that would melt iron, and I saw a lot of that smile when she questioned me. In fact, I warmed to it. Later, I decided I must have been experiencing a hot flash, although I didn't think I was supposed to have those anymore.

Then, suddenly, it was all over. Everyone was gone, including Peters, who was no longer a living creature full of complexities but only a body empty of any sign of life. I did notice that a morgue person had slapped the wig back on his head before they zipped him up in a dark bag and rolled him out. That was kind, I remember thinking.

LORENZA AND I went back to the kitchen after the police and customers left. She sent the staff home on paid leave and told them that she would call within a few days with schedules. Elena offered to stay and clean up. Lorenza kissed her and shooed her out the door after the others. "Go home," she said to Elena. "Get some rest. I'm really going to need you. I'll call you tomorrow afternoon."

Emma, however, she held back.

"I'm sorry," Lorenza said, tears beginning to well up in her eyes. Shock was apparently setting in.

"Why?" Emma's voice was dull. Her eyes looked so dry they could have cracked.

"I think you're going to be out of a job."

Well, bravo, I thought. Normally, Lorenza agonized for days before firing someone.

"After the way I performed tonight, I don't blame you for firing me."

And Emma was even going to make it easy for her! One small point in her favor. I smiled to myself. Since things were going the way I thought they should, I could afford to be generous.

"I didn't say 'fire.' The salad…well, what happened?"

This was not a good turn of events. Emma should have already been permanently on her way out the door after her fiasco tonight.

"I accidentally dropped most of a bottle of olive oil in the bowl I use for mixing the dressing. Instead of dumping it out immediately, I went to get something to clean up the mess, and, when I got back, someone had apparently used it, thinking I was done mixing. It was my fault. I was late getting here and got behind on basic prep like the vinaigrette."

"And the burrito?" I snarled. "Let's not forget the green pea–and–library paste filling Peters was about to wax poetic over."

"Maybe the burrito was okay. No one said it wasn't. Why don't we give it a fair trial and taste the filling." Lorenza gave me what is quaintly referred to, in some works of fiction, as a "significant look."

Emma glanced at the counter, which was still cluttered with food in various stages of preparation. She walked over and started pushing around bowls, plates, and storage containers, opening lids and looking in. "It's not here," she said finally.

"Fancy that!" I muttered.

"Never mind," Lorenza said. "The last thing I'm worried about right now is the damned filling!" And then she started to cry.

To my surprise, Emma went to Lorenza and put her arms around her, very gently hugging and rocking her as if she were a small child. "It's okay. Everything is going to be okay. Just let yourself cry." Her voice dropped into that soothing alto a mother uses when her child has skinned her knee.

After a couple of minutes, Lorenza began to look around for tissues. I handed her a thick, white restaurant napkin. "What in the hell are we going to do now?" she sniffled.

"Close for three days," I said.

"Why three days?" Lorenza and Emma asked in unison.

"In case Peters was right about himself, and he rises from the dead. Then he'll know you took him seriously, and, who knows, you might even get a good review."

"I can't believe you just said that!" But my good Catholic friend began to laugh in spite of herself.

"And if you really think he might rise from the dead and come back, perhaps squid ink pasta should be featured that night," Emma said.

I didn't know our Emma had a sense of humor.

"Why?" Lorenza was always good as a straight man on jokes.

"What better tribute to a food critic than to have the reviewed food in mourning," Emma explained.

"You're both impossible."

I wasn't sure I liked being linked with Emma on anything, but I couldn't resist a low chuckle.

"But seriously, the restaurant is finished. I can't reopen. No one is going to come back to a place where someone died."

"Bull," I snorted. "People like The Lovage. It's not like you poisoned him with the burrito." I hesitated. "Although you just might want to take that off the menu for a while."

"'The Poisoned Burrito'. Sounds like a murder mystery," Lorenza said.

I laughed and glanced up at Emma, who wasn't even smiling. Her face looked yellow in the light.

"You'll need a while to get a new chef. If you let me, I'll stay until you do. I know Elena doesn't want the job, but, if I promise to help her, maybe she will take over until you can get someone else." Emma's voice had taken on a somber tone.

"If you quit because of this, why do you think I'll get any customers back?"

I wanted to jump up and down and shout at Lorenza, "Let her go!"

"I'm not quitting because Peters chose to drop dead in the restaurant. I'm quitting because I failed you tonight."

Yes!

"You think I didn't contribute to this disaster? You think that menu was the best choice I could have made for Peters to review?"

Damn Lorenza and her sense of fairness! On the other hand, I suddenly caught myself saying, "It didn't exactly contain the finest entrées The Lovage has to offer." I didn't want to weigh in on Emma's side, but Lorenza was right. She really could have done better.

"Spoken like a true friend." Lorenza smiled at me. "Look, why should I discount weeks of great cooking for one night of…So you dropped the oil and someone used it for Peters's salad. That was an accident. The burrito may have been a creation of genius that would have swept the salad out of Peters's memory. How do we know?"

"I do know. It was lousy." Emma was looking down at her hands.

"Maybe you should have talked to me first before you tried something new on tonight of all nights. In the future…"

"Look…"

"It was one night."

"Lorenza, you've been wonderful to me. You gave me a chance to get back to doing something I love, and I failed you. How do you know I wouldn't fail you again with the next critic?"

Good point!

"The next one won't be Peters, and there won't be that extra pressure he always brought with him." Then she looked at Emma quietly for a moment. "You really think there will be a next time? You should know."

"You have a superb restaurant. The recipes are wonderful. The atmosphere is great. People love to come here. Yes, there will be a next time. What happened tonight had nothing to do with you or The Lovage. It was all about my inability to deal…"

"And mine," Lorenza said.

Emma suddenly looked very tired and just shook her head as if she couldn't talk any more.

"You have been the perfect chef for The Lovage since you got here. As far as tonight is concerned, I understand about the salad, and we can talk about that burrito another day. In the meantime, I want you to stay. Next time, though, I think we should have Alice do the menu."

"Maybe Alice should do the cooking too," Emma whispered.

"I eat," I said, patting my ample waist. "I don't cook."

So it was settled. Any post-mortem on the burrito would wait. Lorenza decided to close the restaurant for a few days, reopen, and go on, hoping customers would come back.

And Emma was going to stay.

LEAVING THEM TO do whatever they were going to do about cleaning up the kitchen and shutting down, I went into the dark and shadowy dining room to lock up. The shock was wearing off for me too, I guess. I suddenly felt absolutely exhausted. I wanted very much to get home to my very hungry and very pissed cats, crawl into my very empty bed, and fall into a very deep sleep.

I looked around the room. Light from the street colored some of the tables and chairs shades of ghastly yellow. Shadows almost hid others. Eerily, the scene did resemble a deserted stage set. But what was the play? Maybe *Much Ado About Nothing*. I hoped so. I moved tables from one place to another and pulled chairs back. With all the shifting around, I almost couldn't remember where it had all taken place. Almost.

It was then I saw the wristwatch, partially hidden under a table. As I moved one table away from the glow of the streetlight, I saw something flash on the floor. It was one of those watches that you can't tell is a woman's fake Rolex at a distance of twenty feet or so. Irreverent as this admission might be, I have never understood the appeal of the real Rolex, in either the male or female version. They both look like a kid's first effort in machine shop to me. But then, to quote my mother, I never did understand good taste. In any event, if I didn't like the real thing, you can imagine what I thought of the fake.

Anyway, I picked the silly thing up. It was clearly a phony. Even in the reflected light I could see that the silvery color was already wearing off. I rolled it over. It didn't look like the band had broken so I assumed someone had taken it off at dinner and set it aside for some reason or other. I looked around the room, trying to picture who was sitting where, but I had so rearranged everything that I couldn't remember. Besides, someone may have kicked it in all the commotion, so there was no telling which table it had actually belonged to.

Poor soul! Not only had someone had a horrible experience tonight, she had also lost her watch. I wondered if she would call for it after what had happened. I glanced back down at the cheap little thing in my hand. Since I was pretty sure I'd forget about it myself, I decided the average woman would call and retrieve it. To be fair, perhaps she had a sentimental reason for wanting it back despite all the drama this evening. After all, Frances had given me some things I could never bear to lose. Like herself.

I clutched the watch until it cut into my hand. My brain obligingly surrendered the exceptionally vivid image of Frances reaching out to me with her delicate hands through the ghostly pale light in the dining room and immediately began to register this minor but sharp pain instead.

I walked very quickly back toward the bright lights of the kitchen and dumped the watch on the table in front of Lorenza. "Here," I said. "Someone lost this. Better put it in the safe."

I shut my eyes. They burned. "I think we all better go home. If you're as tired as I am, you must be de—worn out."

Lorenza nodded. Emma was staring past Lorenza at the wall behind as if she wanted to ignore both of us. I was getting tired of her, and I was getting tired of being here. "Go home," I told Emma, then took the watch and dumped it in the safe myself. By the time I had finished locking the safe, Emma was gone and Lorenza was waiting for me at the back door.

LORENZA AND I drove home at a speed considerably reduced from the one earlier in the day. That's because I drove. Lorenza was clearly depressed. When I pulled into her driveway and turned off the engine, we sat without speaking for a while, listening to the crickets chirp.

"Can I do anything for you? Make you some tea? Hot chocolate. With marshmallows?" That was a big offer; I hate marshmallows.

Lorenza put her arm around my shoulders and squeezed. "No. I just want to go to bed. Believe it or not, I think I'm going to sleep like a rock tonight. Will you be around tomorrow to talk?"

"What do you think?" I hugged her back. "Just call." And then we got out of the car and each of us walked into her separate house.

CHAPTER 5

NEVER HAVE CATS unless you want to be told what to do when you get home at night. Forget whatever hellish day you might have had in the world of humans; cats just don't care. And don't try to tell me this proves how insensitive the little darlings are.

Cats, you see, are much wiser than people. They know that if you've had an absolutely rotten day at work, for instance, you've probably lost perspective on what's really important—like their dinner and a clean cat box—and they take it as their responsibility to remind you. I've been told that small children have the same sobering effect on one's life, but cats sleep more and the nine o'clock crazies are of shorter duration than the terrible twos.

With all that in mind, you can understand what I expected when I walked into my house that night. Edward and Piers, my two gray stripes, stood a sensible five feet back from the door when I opened it. Having been homeless as kittens, they want nothing to do with the outside world again and make sure they never get too close to it. Instead of soothing purrs and circling furry bodies, I was greeted with the sound from which the word *caterwauling* must have originally come.

Forget that they had three bowls of different kinds of dry food and two bowls of fresh, cool water on the kitchen floor. Forget the heat of the earlier day or the lateness of the current hour. I was inexcusably late with their dinner can, that vile-smelling concoction they certainly don't need but apparently forms a basic part of their routine.

I apologized. Cat owners will understand just how abjectly I apologized. And then I explained why I had been so late. Neither apologies nor excuses really mean a thing to a cat. Cats don't care what you say. They only care about what you do. Nonetheless, I keep hoping that, one of these days, a good story will change their minds.

After the can was opened, divided equally between the two, paper plates put on the floor and the feeding frenzy over, all was finally forgiven. Following a brief but traditional aprés-dinner self-scrub, each jumped up and settled on a respective thigh as I sat in my TV chair, too tired to change my clothes. It was then that I got the soothing purrs.

I MUST HAVE dozed for a bit. The next time I was conscious of anything, the cats had left for a more comfortable and secure sleeping place where they could curl into their usual head-to-tail position, probably in the middle of my bed.

Suddenly, I was wide-awake with a horrible thought. I couldn't remember if anyone had actually locked up The Lovage. I panicked. This was not the time to suffer from memory lapses! I tried to picture what had happened when the three of us left the restaurant. Emma had left first, so I knew she hadn't done it. I couldn't picture whether Lorenza, who had walked out in front of me, had turned back to lock the door. I was pretty sure I hadn't; I almost never do. Mind you, crime is not big news in Livorno, but, after what had happened already tonight, I didn't want the first burglary in town within recent memory to be at The Lovage too.

"Shit!" I said to the blank TV screen and went into the bedroom to change out of my good clothes into something more appropriate for locking up a restaurant after midnight: gardening pants and an old T-shirt with paint stains.

FORTUNATELY, MY CAR is used to driving on automatic pilot. It does it five days a week when it takes me into San Francisco at the

ungodly hour I have to leave for work. And it truly did yeoman
service going down the hill in this effort at crime prevention. I was
shocked into full alertness, however, when I swung into the back
driveway of The Lovage and almost rear-ended a white Sentra.

"Bloody hell," I said, slamming on the brakes. I looked carefully
at the car. It wasn't Lorenza's. Hers had a dent in the rear where…
Well, never mind. It wasn't hers, so it had to be Emma's.

I was pissed. "If she remembered to come and lock up, the least
she could have done was call me," I muttered as I lumbered out of
my car. Of course, why should she have called me, but I was not in
a reasonable frame of mind.

If Emma had come to lock up, there was no sign of her. I couldn't
see any light on in the restaurant. Then I saw what appeared to be a
dark shadow moving away from the Dumpster.

"Emma?"

I'm blind at night, and middle age hasn't helped what little
night vision I once did have, but I was sure someone was there.

"Emma?"

I felt my way as quickly as I could toward the path leading to the
back porch. The shadow was moving even faster.

"Emma!" I shouted a third time at the figure I now heard crash-
ing through the vegetation toward the front of the building.

"Jesus!" My foot caught, and I began to fall, just catching myself
before I landed smack on top of a large soft mound right at the bottom of the back stairs.

You've heard of hair standing up on the back of the neck? Well,
mine definitely did. Seeing one dead body is enough to last anyone
a lifetime. Frances had been my first, Peters my second. I felt I had
been overblessed, so to speak. But my eyes were finally adjusting to
the dark, and, right under my feet I was pretty sure was a potential third. I stepped back and slowly knelt on the ground. Gingerly,
I reached out. My hand touched cloth. Underneath, the body was
warm. I bent closer. The head was just to the right of my hand. The
hair looked blond. It was Emma.

I'm not a screamer. On the other hand, vomiting was not out of the question. Fortunately, the body moved, and I heard some sound akin to a soft groan.

Never let it be said that fat women can't run. I probably broke a Guinness world record in leaping up the back stairs, through a locked door, and dialing 911 before taking a breath. I was even coherent. I even remembered the address.

I turned on all the kitchen lights, grabbed a flashlight, and started back down the stairs. I flicked the light on the body. It was definitely Emma. There was dark stuff on her light jacket. Lots of it. Most likely it was blood, and I had absolutely no knowledge of first aid. I couldn't even pretend to help her.

"Where is that ambulance, damn it!" In helpless frustration, I began to flash the light around the area of the shrubs and garden as if that would help Emma, dead or dying, below me. And if I thought I would see whoever did it, well, whoever else had been there certainly hadn't stayed around for any standing ovation.

I passed the light over the Dumpster. No one had taken the time to dump the evening garbage, but something had been tossed in. Because strange things pique my curiosity, I took a quick glance. It looked like a shattered earthenware bowl.

Just as I was beginning to take a closer look, the ambulance squealed around the corner from the main street and came to a screeching halt behind my car. And right behind the ambulance came a police car. I started to laugh nervously. "Why, we're creating our own little daisy chain!" I caught myself thinking. "Oh, shut up!" I said out loud and centered the flashlight on Emma. I really didn't want the paramedics to lose any time finding her. They didn't. One even waved a thanks in my direction.

A stocky, indistinct figure jumped from the police car and moved quickly toward where the paramedics were clustered around Emma. After a few minutes, Detective Thompson then strode up the steps, took me quite gently by the arm, and aimed me back into the kitchen.

"Didn't we just meet earlier this evening?" she asked, as she held a chair for me to sit down.

I looked up at her face and decided that smile of hers would not only melt iron but also turn the blackest heart red. My heart was already a healthy shade of pink.

"This has been quite an experience for you," she continued. "Do you need something to drink?"

"Is she okay?" I heard the ambulance drive off with that horrible wail. I shuddered.

"She's alive."

"Where's she going?"

"County," Thompson said. "Don't worry. She's lost blood, but she's young and County handles stab wounds very well. They should. They have lots of practice."

I winced.

"She's a friend of yours?"

I was beginning to sweat, a cold sweat. I didn't know if that meant I was going to feel better or worse. At the moment, I felt lousy.

"Her name is Emma Stilwell. She's the chef here. You talked to her earlier. Her employer is Lorenza Galli. She has health insurance."

"What?"

My head was swimming.

"Are you feeling all right?"

The chair flew over backward, but I made it to the sink before I threw up. Detective Thompson helped me back to the chair and gave me a damp dishcloth to wipe my face.

"Sorry about that," I said, feeling better but still shaky.

"You're not the first person to react like that in similar situations." Her voice had changed to a cool and cautious professional tone.

"I didn't do whatever to her," I snapped, missing her previous warmth and inexplicably resenting the absence.

"I didn't suggest you had. But maybe you can tell me what happened?"

"I'm not sure I know," I replied, swallowing to keep from gagging.

"Can you tell me what you saw then?"

I didn't want to think about any of the night anymore, let alone talk about what had just happened. In fact, I really wanted to tell the good detective to go to hell, but she had such a hopeful look on her face as she handed me another damp dishcloth, that I was beginning to feel more civic-minded.

"I really didn't see much, besides nearly tripping on Emma lying there." I retched slightly but dryly. "Although, when I first got here, I thought I saw someone running from the Dumpster, away from me, and toward the path that leads along the side of the restaurant to the front. I assumed it was Emma and shouted her name, but no one answered. I started to run after—whomever, and that's when I tripped over Emma."

"Do you remember on which side the figure was running?"

I waved my hand in the general vicinity. Detective Thompson looked at me carefully for a long moment, got up, and disappeared out the back door. I buried my face in the soothing coolness of the damp cloth.

I have no idea how long she was gone, but I felt her return before I saw her standing over me.

"You said you thought the figure running away was your friend."

I nodded, ignoring the "friend" bit.

"You didn't think the figure was a man?"

"I don't understand."

"The person running away was small enough that you thought it was a woman?"

"I don't think I thought about it. I just assumed it was Emma. I guess I really couldn't say now."

"Why did you chase the person you thought was Emma?"

"I don't know. I guess I just wanted to stop her. I didn't understand why she was running away. Perhaps I had frightened her, and I certainly hadn't meant to do that." Or, to be honest, maybe I trusted her so little after what she had already done to Lorenza's business, I suspected her of coming down to do something else to the restaurant, and I didn't want her to escape. I decided I didn't want to say that. It wasn't pertinent to Emma getting stabbed and would just sound petty.

Although Thompson may have thought my explanation made about as much sense as my chasing some unknown person after midnight in a dark and fairly deserted location, she let the answer pass.

"And why were you here?" she asked.

At least I could answer that one easily. "I couldn't remember if anyone had locked the back door to the restaurant. Since I was still up, I came down to check. The owner is a good friend and neighbor, so I have a key. You can verify with Lorenza—Galli, the owner."

"Was the restaurant locked?"

I hesitated a moment. "Yes. Yes, the back door was. I had to unlock it to get to the phone. I haven't checked the front, but I did lock that myself before we all went home." Then before she could ask, I added, "That was about elevenish."

Thompson disappeared toward the dining area and came back a short while later.

"Has anyone broken in?" I asked.

"No broken windows, and the front door was locked."

"I didn't check the safe." I started to get up, got dizzy, and fell back into the chair. "It's over there." I gestured.

Thompson, hands on hips, gave it a visual once over. "No one's blown it up."

"Goody." I started to laugh. "By the way, I don't know anything much about Emma. I just met her tonight. You better ask Lorenza that sort of thing."

"I think you've had enough tonight anyway. We can talk later.

Do you have someone I can call to take you home?"

"It's all right. I can drive. My cats haven't learned. Not that they're not smart enough. They just aren't interested. You know cats." I started to get out of the chair again with no more luck than the first time.

"I'm getting you a ride home. Which is your car?" As she helped me up and walked me toward the door, she gave me another one of those wonderful smiles. I felt a rush of heat rise from my neck and knew my face was flushing red. My stomach might be settling, but I really did need to talk to my gynecologist about those hot flashes.

CHAPTER 6

LORENZA LET ME sleep until nine the next morning before she called. Actually, Edward and Piers had let me sleep until seven, which was late for them. I still felt gritty from fatigue, but at least I'd bathed and had some coffee.

"Are you awake?" Lorenza rather inexplicably asked when I answered the phone. She sounded about as alert as I felt.

"No," I answered.

She laughed.

I wasn't joking.

"Did the police call you about last night?" I asked.

"Sometime around two A.M."

"You know about Emma then."

"I can't believe this all happened the same night. Peters dead. Emma nearly so. Poor Emma!"

Typical Lorenza, worrying about someone else as if nothing had happened to her last night, like a famous food critic dropping dead in her restaurant and her head cook stabbed shortly thereafter.

"You mean 'poor you.' Now you're short a chef after everything else that happened yesterday."

"I'm not in the morgue, and I'm not in the hospital. Considering those options, I think I'm doing okay."

She had a point.

"Want to come to County with me?"

"Sure." I hesitated. "You mean you're going to see Emma?"

"Who else could I mean?"

With Lorenza, you never knew.

"I'm just surprised they're letting her have visitors," I said.

"I called earlier. The nurse said Emma'd lost a lot of blood and was unconscious for a while. She's doing well, considering, but we can't stay long."

"And which of us is the mother this time?"

Hospitals are only supposed to give out information to close family members. In the Bay Area, however, the term *family* is often both compassionately and broadly interpreted according to the spirit of the law, whatever the strict letter might say. Nonetheless, Lorenza and I have been known to, shall we say, make up a relationship when needed just in case.

"Neither. I told them I was her employer. Emma's never mentioned any family, so I assumed she didn't have any close by, and that's what I told the nurse. You better be prepared to play aunt though. I think they'll buy a blond niece with a red-haired aunt better than an aunt with olive skin and black hair."

No one's ever said you've got to like everyone in your family.

"Alice?"

"I'm here. Just thinking. I'm surprised there's no swarm about the hive."

"And that's supposed to mean...?"

"Boyfriends."

"She lives alone. I've never seen her with anyone, family or otherwise. She did list a friend on her employment papers, Antonio Petroni, but I haven't been able to reach him. I didn't notice until now that she hadn't put down a phone number or address for him."

"Probably the boyfriend."

"I don't think so. I've never seen him. And why not give me a way to contact him?"

"Perhaps not surprising if our Emma was being discreet. What do you know about her anyway?"

"That's just what that nice detective asked."

I was glad this was one hot flash Lorenza didn't see. "I'm not trying to solve a crime. Only curious."

"Well, she's a good cook."

Could've fooled me.

"She owned her own restaurant several years ago."

In the subbasement of the Transbay Bus Terminal?

"She got her degree in culinary science from City College in San Francisco."

"Hey, wait a minute! What happened to the restaurant?"

"It failed."

"I'll bet. Drugs, alcohol, or just plain incompetence?"

"Alice, lots of restaurants fail in San Francisco. It's a tough market. And what do you mean by 'drugs, alcohol, or just plain incompetence'? That's a nasty remark, and so was your tone of voice. What could you possibly have against her anyway?"

"Last night is what I have against her. She'd have ruined you if Peters had lived to write his review."

"I think Peters dropping dead…"

"Restaurants have survived customers dropping dead of natural causes, but a bad review would have killed The Lovage, which you said yourself. And from what I saw, Peters would have been right to pan the dinner. The salad was America's answer to the next oil crisis, and God knows what Emma did to the burrito."

"Bend a little, Alice. The salad was an honest case of nerves and some bad timing. The burrito remains an unknown. Before last night, Emma performed professionally and damned well. I can't count the number of times customers have complimented her meals—more compliments than when I cooked, I can tell you."

I didn't want to argue with Lorenza. Both of us were tired and on edge. Admittedly, Emma had irritated me even before the Peters incident, in fact, from the moment I set eyes on her. If I were honest with myself, my dislike for her was probably just a tiny bit irrational, and no matter how bad the salad, she certainly hadn't deserved getting stabbed.

"Okay, I'll stuff it. When do you want to see her?"

"After lunch. Maybe we both need naps."

I hung up and went out into my garden. Gardens are utterly peaceful. That's why I go there when life becomes too complicated or I have a problem that's more than I can deal with. Even if I don't come back inside with answers, at least I'm refreshed enough to try again.

I raised my face to the sun, shut my eyes, and concentrated on the buzzing of insects, an occasional bird twitter,…and the distant roar of cars on the freeway. The air was heating up, promising another blistering day.

How sad, I thought. Maybe I had become just like anyone else who rushed into rural living. Maybe I too had begun to think I'd escaped all the evils of society, forgetting that I had just as much social evil in me as anybody. Here I was, pointing an accusing finger at Emma and acting as if I had good reason to suspect and dislike her when the only thing really wrong was probably just some bad chemistry between us. I had given myself credit for better sense than to jump to conclusions solely out of ignorance. Wake up call!

I opened my eyes, took in a deep breath of sweet, flower-scented air, and let it out very slowly. If I wasn't better than that, at least I could act as if I were, I decided, and looked around my garden. Maybe a bouquet of cornflowers and baby ferns would help soothe and cheer Emma.

I'd even pick off any bugs, the uglier ones at least.

CHAPTER 7

I DROVE. GIVEN our comparative lack of rest, I decided that staying awake at the wheel that afternoon might not be Lorenza's strong suit. At least my five hours of sleep were vastly superior to her zilch.

We talked on the way. Lorenza is not one to stay down for long. By the time we were halfway to the hospital, she was feeling much more optimistic and almost convinced The Lovage would survive. It didn't take long to get her thinking about fall soups and spicy North African dishes for the new season. By the time I pulled into the hospital parking lot, she was in good enough spirits to cheer anyone up, including Emma.

And Emma obviously needed it. I would have sworn she had been crying when we walked in. One hand was pressed to her forehead, covering her eyes. When she heard us, she looked up and smiled. Although her eyes and nose were both red, her smile did look genuine and clearly included both of us.

I felt guilty as hell. She looked so pale lying there, bandaged heavily with one arm in a sling.

"You saved my life, you know. I won't forget that." She reached out and squeezed my hand.

My guilt trip just doubled, and I felt my face flush vividly. "Here," I squawked, shoving the bouquet toward her nose, "I thought you might like these."

"They're beautiful!" Her eyes sparkled for just a second before she dropped my hand and grabbed at her shoulder. "Ouch!"

"Are you all right?" Lorenza asked.

Dropping the flowers, I reached over and touched her uninjured shoulder ever so gently and sympathetically. It was then I realized her queue of hair was gone and the back of her neck was also bandaged. Lousy way to get a haircut.

I shook my head. She really had come very close to death last night, whether or not I had actually saved her life simply by arriving when I did. Suddenly I wanted to hug her but patted her free arm instead. "Do you need something?" I asked.

"I'm okay. Really. I just get sharp pains once in awhile." Then she looked at the flowers, which had fallen into her lap. "But these are so beautiful, Alice. Where did you get such a delightful mix?" She turned the bouquet every which way and actually seemed to enjoy the riot of blues, greens, and yellows (I had thrown in a few yellow mini-roses on a whim) that I had hurriedly put together.

"From my garden."

"You grew these? You must have a wonderful garden."

"Best herbs in the county too." Lorenza had been standing on the other side of Emma's bed, where I could see her having a quiet chuckle over my obvious discomfort. At least she had kept my snide comments about her chef to herself. "I thought I'd told you. Alice is my prime supplier for those. She also grows a lot of tomatoes, onions, and zucchini for The Lovage. Whatever is in season. It's all organic too."

"Of course! I'm sorry. You did tell me some time ago, Lorenza." She shook her head as if to clear it, then looked up at me. "And you brought those boxes of herbs and vegetables yesterday." Emma winced again and dropped her eyes.

There was something about this gesture that made me wonder if the current pain had less to do with the physical and more to do with something remembered. Either way, I decided some distracting chitchat might be helpful.

"By the way, Lorenza had some fabulous recipe ideas on the way to the hospital. You won't starve or have to cook for ages once you're out of here. I know from experience that she loves a good guinea pig. I'll be happy to turn the honor over to you."

"You make it sound like a very unpleasant experience." Lorenza looked hurt.

"Considering how little I cook, have I ever lost an ounce? Have I ever been less than eager for a Lorenza-cooked meal?"

"No."

"There you have it. You, Emma, are about to join the ranks of the well fed. And should you need anything from the grocery store, give me a call. My cats love it when I run errands and give them some much needed peace and quiet."

That got a laugh. "Your cats need peace and quiet?"

Lorenza's eyes rolled skyward. "Alice has a nice collection of classical CDs too."

Her quick change of subject was deliberate. She sometimes thinks I become a bit daft when I start talking about the cats, and she gets very protective of my reputation. I have long suspected she is secretly a dog person.

I smiled innocently at Lorenza and continued. "Yes, I do. The plants like the music. That's why they grow so well. I usually leave the windows open so the plants, cats, and I all can enjoy the music while I garden." I wasn't about to help Lorenza improve my image. She shot me her most dramatic warning look.

"What music in particular?" Emma asked gamely.

"Violin. String quartets. Orchestral. Even opera on occasion. Lots, actually."

"And what do your cats prefer?"

For that comment I could almost have liked her. She was certainly getting into the spirit of this. "'The Tallis Scholars,' but nothing much written after Elizabeth I died. At least, Edward, the oldest, doesn't. I played one of Nirvana's albums in a moment of curiosity once, and he hid under the bed for two days. Piers was a shade more liberal. He just tossed his dinner on my bedspread."

Emma laughed, and her skin tone began to take on a healthier shade of pink. "I must meet your cats—and see your garden."

"You will," Lorenza said quickly, hoping to shut me up before I continued on with more tales of Edward and Piers.

I had no reason to be cooperative. After all, Emma was clearly enjoying my outrageous cat stories. "And they even like several of the vegetables I grow, although Edward prefers grapes."

"I think we've probably stayed long enough." Lorenza was getting nervous. "Alice, why don't you get something to put the flowers in, and then we can be on our way. Emma, call me when you need a ride home. Don't worry about the medical costs and income. I'm checking with workers' comp on what they cover in medical. The health insurance covers the hospital, and I did your paperwork for state disability. Just need your signature. Here's a pen. And The Lovage is reopening. Call me when you feel up to a little work. I need to talk over some menus."

From the look on her face, I was pretty sure Emma was going to start crying again. Lorenza was better at handling that. I went out to find water and a vase for the flowers.

LORENZA WAS CLEARLY in a good mood. She bounded across the parking lot toward the car like a thirsty antelope scenting water. I was bouncing after her with the efficiency of a deflating basketball. "Slow down, will you?" I panted loudly.

"Was I walking too fast? Sorry." Lorenza stopped, turned, and smiled. "Look. Another one of your favorite cars." She was pointing at a red Miata one row back of my ever-faithful green Toyota. "Must be popular little things. You really should get one."

I glanced at the car. The woman in the driver's seat pulled down the visor. "Stop pointing, Lorenza. I see it. I have no plans to trade in my precious car for something with no trunk space. I need to haul stuff."

"Get a truck for the free-range chicken manure. You need a Miata so you'll have something to drive that doesn't smell of what you've just hauled."

"Don't insult my car. She may stall and make us both walk home."

She laughed.

We didn't talk much on the way back. The afternoon was hot, my car has no air conditioning, and Lorenza fell victim to fatigue. She was asleep almost before we were back on the freeway and began to snore loudly with a slight smile on her face. It was an endearing sight, and I squeezed her hand gently.

"You're a good woman, Lorenza Galli," I whispered. Despite the state disability, the health plan offered by a small business, and maybe workers' comp, there would probably be lots of expenses Lorenza wouldn't want Emma to worry about. That could be one hell of a debt my kind friend had just taken on. I hoped Emma was worth it.

CHAPTER 8

WHETHER OR NOT I really had been having more hot flashes recently, Lorenza had been hounding me for weeks about getting my annual physical. Since she had had enough to worry about of late, I decided to chop this one thing off her list and let her win the argument. Besides, the only way I could get her to shut up about it was to give in.

Like many women, my primary physician is a gynecologist, and, like a rational person, I believe in taking responsibility for my health by doing all that preventive maintenance stuff like annual physicals. But I'm also an emotional person, and I hate going to doctors. Physicals are particularly unpleasant because it means the annual pelvic.

I go to one of those legalistic-sounding groups called Inness, Ardent & Smith. I call them Innards Inc. My personal physician was Smith, who had decided to retire earlier in the year. Now I not only had to face the dreaded pelvic, I also had to do so with a stranger.

And Dr. Smith had been the only man in the group. Of course we all know the majority of doctors are quite professional and frankly could give a good goddamn about what any of us looks like. I mean, it is really irrelevant to them whether we're attractive, dress well, or even have matching shoes. Therefore, the only thing on our minds should be whether he/she/whichever is competent enough to see when something should or shouldn't be on the body part under examination.

That's the rational approach. But, when you're lying there stark naked in that graceless position with your feet in the stirrups, you find you care very much what you look like and who's looking. Frankly, I would rather die than have a woman see me like that. So, while it may be unusual for a lesbian to prefer a male doctor, I don't care. This is one time I want a man.

At work on Monday, I ground my teeth and called Innards Inc. for an appointment. I tried to think positively. Maybe, in the interests of gender diversity, they had added another man to the group. If his name began with another letter, would I have to drop "Innards"?

"Doctors' office?"

I was trapped. I suppose I could have hung up, but I'm a proud woman. Besides, I was doing this for Lorenza. With luck, maybe so many women were trying to get pregnant that Innards wouldn't have a free appointment for months.

"Doctors Inness and Ardent are booked up this week."

"That's okay! I'll..."

"But Dr. Swan has joined us and could see you Friday at one o'clock?"

Damn! Well, it is the Irish who are supposed to have all the luck, not their cousin Scots. I graciously agreed to time and date.

The moment I hung up, I realized I hadn't the vaguest idea whether Dr. Swan was a man or a woman.

DON'T ASK ME what I do for a living. Suffice it to say that I work for a multipurpose company in a department whose function is inexplicable and within which I have an indescribable job with an equally indefinable title. Fortunately, I have always done sufficiently well not to be fired for incompetence. On the other hand, I have also never had adequate whatever or known enough of the right whomevers to get promoted. The job provides health insurance and a decent enough living. My tastes, however, have never run to BMWs or a vacation home in some ski resort. I'll be there until I die. Or the company goes belly up, whichever comes first.

As expected, the workweek was filled with the clients from hell. And, of course, Dr. Swan turned out to be a woman. Not only was she a woman, she was a slender, bright young thing, right out of some high-powered residency, with dark brown eyes, flawless café-au-lait skin, gold wire glasses, and black hair done in an intricate weave. Everything about her just screamed "class, money, and style." When I saw her walk into the examining room, I clutched the flimsy paper wrapper that failed to cover me by at least ten inches.

It ripped.

She smiled sympathetically.

I felt myself blush as red as my hair, then dutifully lay back and thought, as it were, of England.

The entire experience rated an early dinner at my favorite restaurant in the city, Walton Square.

WALTON SQUARE IS sparkling glass, polished wood, burnished brass, and fresh food. The menus defy description, being neither ethnic, Californian, nor American. Whatever all that means anyway. The dishes are art on a plate, but this chef has never forgotten that food is intended to feed people as well as look pretty.

I know Joan, the owner and chef, a bit, although she's really a friend of Lorenza. She also reminds me a lot of Elena: tiny and quick-witted, black-haired and sharpfeatured, but a veritable cyclone of enthusiasm. Her food and the atmosphere she's created in her restaurant bring me back again and again, especially when I need comforting.

As I came through the door, I got a big smile and wave from Joan, who was in the open kitchen. It was too early for the dinner crowd and too late for the lunchers. My favorite table in the corner by the great carved bird, where I could usually people-watch in peace, was free.

A half bottle of my favorite white Burgundy opened and poured in front of me, I went over the menu. Even though I joined Lorenza in the vegetarian diet a long time ago as an attempt to stop the massive weight gain I suffered after Frances died, I love to read the entire selection at Walton Square as a treat to my senses before I finally order. Most of the servers know me and give me time to browse.

"How's the wild mushroom ragoût with asparagus and polenta?" I asked, when the server came over. That was a rhetorical question here. Besides, I have yet to meet a mushroom I wasn't wild about.

"A great dish by a new member of our staff. Absolutely luscious."

"Sold. And I'll have the chocolate mousse torte with mocha ganache for dessert." Wasp-waisted Dr. Swan and her not-so-subtle hints about my weight could go to hell in a handbasket tonight.

As expected, the meal was texture-rich food with earth colors and guaranteed, with each bite of fresh taste, to comfort all those areas of body and soul that had been wounded in the course of a mindless weekly grind. Like a large cat, I half-closed my eyes and savored everything slowly.

Once the last crumb of the torte was gone, I felt renewed. I paid the check and wandered over to the kitchen to give the chef a hello from Lorenza as well as my rave review on the ragoût and torte.

"Really bad luck about Peters croaking at The Lovage," she said. "But Lorenza will pull out of it. It's not the first time somebody died in a restaurant."

"At least the newspaper reports were pretty decent. They made it pretty clear he probably died from a heart attack."

"I have to admit I'm not too sad to see him off the food-reviewing circuit. I was lucky. The last time he reviewed me, my co-owner husband was still alive, although just barely."

Maybe Lorenza should have had George stuffed and put on the porch outside the restaurant to greet Peters.

"I'm just sorry Peters died though. He would have been much more fun writing the society page," she continued.

"True!" I laughed. "By the way, that mushroom ragoût was out of this world. The recipe is one of your best yet."

"That wasn't mine. It was Tony's. Why don't you tell him yourself? He'd love to hear it, and he's on break." She pointed in the direction of the banquet room in the back, which can't be seen except from the kitchen area.

As I bent over the counter between the kitchen and the seating area, I saw two men through the open door, talking with their heads close together and hands touching. I would have sworn one was Peters's former secretary. The other, facing me more directly and dressed in chef's white, looked for all the world like a miniature Peters minus hairpiece.

"What did you say his name was?" I asked, as an ill-defined little light began to flash in my head.

"Tony? Antonio. Antonio Petroni. He came here about a month ago. Fabulously creative with food."

"Really," I said, as I walked around the counter and toward the open door of the banquet room.

CHAPTER 9

EVEN IN SAN FRANCISCO, gay men will drop hands if surprised by someone they don't know. And that's sad. Seems it's okay for men to go to war and slaughter each other with immense creativity and cost to the taxpayer, but if a man shows public love or tenderness toward another, especially if they aren't related, that's "wussy," questionable, and sometimes bordering on the illegal. We have, however, come a long way from my youth. I actually saw a father hug his adult son the other day. I almost cheered out loud.

Notwithstanding, the Peters look-alike and the man I was now sure was the food critic's former secretary did drop hands when I came into the banquet room. I guess I had interrupted something important because the milk of human kindness was distinctly lacking in the ex-secretary's glare when he turned and looked at me. In fact, had his eyes been Uzis, I'd have been instant pulverized protein.

"I'm Alice McDoughall," I said as calmly as I could and focusing my attention on the chef. "I understand from Joan that you did the wild mushroom ragoût this afternoon. I just wanted to tell you it was wonderful."

You'd have thought I had just given him the Chef of the Year award. His eyes brimmed, then overflowed with tears. "Thank you," he said. "You're more than kind. You have no idea how much that means right now."

The secretary continued to glare at me.

I was beginning to get annoyed with this, but, in the interest of finding out if this Antonio Petroni knew our Emma Stilwell, I tried to swallow the righteous indignation of the totally innocent. "Sorry if I interrupted something," I cooed at the secretary.

He brought his fist down so hard the table jumped.

I jumped.

"Damn!" he said, shot up out of his chair, and stormed out.

I looked at the chef. The chef was looking at the back of his departing friend with an incomprehensible tenderness. Then he smiled. I wasn't sure that was the response I would have had to what had just happened, but I decided to go along.

"Did I say something wrong?" I asked.

"No. Just ignore John. He's upset about something and is in a bit of a temper about it. That's all."

I looked at the small crack in the table left by John's fist. I didn't think I would have called that the result of just "a bit of temper." On the other hand, since no one's head had gotten broken, especially mine, I opted to be charitable.

"I guess I would be pretty edgy too if I had just seen my boss drop dead next to me," I said.

Antonio Petroni's smile disappeared. The tears began to flow in earnest. Then the poor man began to sob.

I blinked in utter confusion. Then I reached over and took his hand. "I'm doing really great in the sensitivity department. I have no idea how, but I just managed to upset you too! Whatever I said wrong, I'm very sorry."

He squeezed my hand and then reached for a wad of tissues from his back pocket. "It's not your fault," he sniffled. "You wouldn't have known."

"Known what?"

"John's boss, as you called him, is—was—my dad."

That tentative little light bulb which had begun to flicker in my head at the name of Antonio Petroni just exploded into a blinding mushroom cloud.

"Dad? Dad! You mean Arthur Peters was your father?"

He nodded.

"Oh," I said, falling heavily into the secretary's vacated chair, "I am so very sorry!"

CHAPTER 10

THE TELEPHONE WAS bleeping off the hook when I walked in the door later that evening. I dropped everything in the middle of the floor, ignored two pairs of glaring green eyes, and picked it up.

"Alice McDoughall?" The voice was warm and familiar. "Angel Thompson, here. Detective Thompson?"

"Of course," I sighed. Angel? How utterly charming!

"I tried to call your friend, Lorenza, but couldn't reach her. She said I should call you if I couldn't catch her. The autopsy results are in."

My image of Thompson as a smiling Cupid and me as Psyche, together on a soft bed of angel feathers, imploded irretrievably into a black hole.

"Ah, yes, the autopsy results." I began to fan myself vigorously.

"I thought she better know."

"Know…?"

"Peters died of a heart attack, all right, but there is also evidence that he was suffering from a severe allergic reaction to something he ate at dinner. An argument might be made that the allergic reaction helped bring on the heart attack."

"What could he have possibly eaten? Lorenza always lists any ingredients known to cause food allergies, like peanuts." Surely it wasn't the olive oil. Maybe it was just his own gall. The fanning hadn't helped, and I was feeling both hot and testy.

"Not peanuts. Fava beans."

"Never heard of them."

"Ever see the movie *The Silence of the Lambs?*"

"Too gruesome for my taste. But I thought the guy liked meat, ah, not veggies."

"He did, but he suggested favas might be a nice side dish to go with…"

I swallowed audibly.

Detective Thompson laughed sympathetically.

I took a deep breath. "Okay, so tell me about this bean."

"A broad bean. You've probably seen them. Fresh, they're green. Canned, they're brown."

Green pea and brown library paste came immediately to mind. "Really! Related to the castor bean by any chance? I remember that's poisonous."

"No, but fresh favas can be highly toxic to some men of Mediterranean ancestry. Usually males anyway. Some of them have a genetic enzyme deficiency that can make them either very sick or even kill them in extreme situations if they eat the uncooked bean."

"Are you saying Peters was killed by eating favas?"

"He had a heart condition. We don't know yet how severe his allergy was. The family has been notified, and we're getting more information from Peters's doctor."

"A little obscure, isn't it? I mean, this isn't your common peanut allergy or something similar."

"Actually, there is a lot of ancient literature on the problem. The Romans considered favas to be unlucky. Pythagoras claimed the bean contained the souls of the dead."

"You're certainly up on your favas." She was almost waxing poetic on the subject. For just the flash of a second, I was actually jealous of the poor bean under discussion.

"I should be. I'm Italian."

"You're kidding! With a name like Thompson?"

"My husband's name. I was born Angelica Grandi. I shortened the first to Angel…"

Husband? I was so stunned I almost dropped the phone, losing track of the conversation and not drifting back until she was saying "…he became a doctor. I call him the Angel of Mercy and he calls me the Angel of…"

I suddenly found my voice. "Death," I said softly.

"Right."

The brief silence echoed in my ears like a loud, tolling bell. Husband! Then she continued as if nothing of significance had just been said. "It's strange, though. Peters wasn't Italian or anything like it."

"Yes he was." I swallowed to clear my dry throat. "I just met his son. Arthur Peters was really Arturo Petroni."

"Shit!" said the Angel of Death.

CHAPTER 11

MOST PEOPLE, WHEN they reach middle age, seem to look back sadly and longingly at all the audacious things they did, think they did, or think they should have done in their youth. Not I. For me, it had been sufficient adventure to move from San Francisco, where I was born, to Livorno, several miles to the north, and buy a house.

Oh, I'm sure some would call me a real daring '60s radical for living openly with my female lover. But to Frances and me, living as a couple was no more "radical" than it would have been had she been Frank and we were able to marry.

That's a long way around to say I have never been one for daring acts or adventures, real or imaginary. But now I was beginning to think that an adventure, thrilling or not, was exactly what I was in the middle of, and I wasn't any too happy about it.

As soon as I finished talking to Thompson, I called all over town for Lorenza. I finally found her with Carlo, the greengrocer.

"I don't care what Carlo's problem with eggplant quality is," I shouted. "Come to the house. Now!"

A few minutes later, I heard the telltale squeal of Lorenza's brakes as she pulled into her driveway. I quickly opened a bottle of wine.

There was no way to break the news gently, and she was, to put it mildly, beyond indignation when I told her what Thompson had told me.

"Alice, I made the burrito filling myself early that morning. There were no fava beans in it. And I would never serve favas without listing them as an ingredient. Maybe the allergy is rare in most parts of the country but not in Italian communities. I know they make some people sick. They gave my father abdominal pain. So they couldn't have been in anything Peters ate that night. There were no beans in the salad, and you don't put favas into a burrito. He must have eaten them someplace else." She gestured wildly with a half-full glass of red wine.

I watched the wineglass and wondered how I felt about cabernet polka dots on my white kitchen curtains. Maybe I could live with one or two.

"Tell that to Petroni père and fils," I said.

"Who?"

"Arthur Peters was actually a not-so-nice Italian boy by the name of Arturo Petroni. He has a son, Antonio. You know. Antonio Petroni? Ring any bells?"

"No."

"Ding! Dong! Antonio Petroni just happens to share the same name as Emma's emergency contact listed on your employment thing."

"I don't understand what—"

"And Emma's good friend, Antonio, son of Arturo, has an even better friend in John, former secretary to Arturo, father of Antonio."

The wineglass was now swinging in circles. "You're a veritable treasure trove of incomprehensible information, Alice. Where in the hell do you think you're leading with all this anyway?" Lorenza's impatient expression told me she had decided one of two things: I must have made this up, or I was pulling her leg for some inexplicably insane reason.

Believe me, I would far rather have faced her short-lived but gale force fury by confessing to either than have laid out the implications here. I didn't think county forensics had made a mistake about which meal had contained the favas. It was clear to me that the otherwise inexplicable appearance of the beans in the allergic

Peters's burrito took on a rather sinister aspect when you attached a few facts: the Tony who was close enough to Emma to be her emergency contact was also the son of Peters and coincidentally had a lover with violent tendencies who was Peters's secretary. I saw the potential here for a suspicious collusion for some yet undefined purpose.

On the other hand, I didn't want to sound like I was leading a one-person vendetta against a woman who was in the hospital, suffering from an almost fatal stab wound, either. Lorenza already knew I disliked Emma. She was used to my instant takes on people based solely on the logic of my incomprehensible psyche. That I was sometimes right—or at least partially…but that argument never flew with Lorenza. If I didn't handle this carefully, she would dismiss my concerns as extreme, just as she had my early dislike of her new chef, and refuse to listen.

The wineglass did another full circle.

"Lorenza, will you put that glass down!"

Lorenza was not amused. "I'm still waiting for you to be more forthcoming with something resembling intelligible details."

"Okay, it all started when I had dinner at Walton Square. By the way, you got a big 'hello' from—"

"Alice! You're the one who insisted I come up here immediately, and you're the one who's suggesting there's a major point here. What is it?"

"I'm not sure how to explain this."

"Great. For this, I left Carlo alone with the eggplant problem. My menu for tomorrow might as well include your cats' leftovers if I don't get—"

I had no choice but to surge blindly ahead. "Okay, fact of interest number one: Emma listed Antonio Petroni, who just happens to be Peters's son, as the person to contact on her employment papers with you. Did she tell you that she knew Peters's son?"

"No."

"Don't you think it's odd that Emma tells you she messed up

because she was nervous about the big, bad critic when she was so close to the guy's son that she lists him as virtual next of kin?"

"Emma never claimed she did anything out of the way that night because of nerves. I made that assumption."

"But you suggested you knew she wasn't exactly a big fan of Peters. Is she?"

"She was definitely unhappy about Peters coming to review us. She was quite clear about that."

"So don't you think it was odd she never told you she knew his son?"

"Just one damned second! You're telling me that some guy by the name of Antonio Petroni is the son of Arthur Peters? Explain to me how you made this great leap of faith with two entirely different names?"

I poured Lorenza another glass of wine. To hell with white curtains.

"Arthur Peters was really Arturo Petroni. According to the son, Peters changed his name after he had some fight with his family. Tony changed his own back after a fight with his father. But you're getting away from my question. Don't you think it's strange Emma never told you she knew—"

"Not especially. Maybe the son is different from the father." Lorenza glared at me. Then she smiled. "And just because she might know the son doesn't mean she knows the father."

I opted to ignore that last remark and surged ahead. "Tony works at Walton Square. He did a really nice thing with mushrooms. When I told Joan, she suggested I tell him personally. He and I had quite a little chat about daddy after he told me Peters was his father." For the moment, I decided to omit the crack in the table left by Tony's boyfriend.

"And…"

"Among the many fascinating things he told me, which I shall fully recount when you haven't eggplant on the brain, was the little fact about his father's extreme allergy to fava beans. Seems one of

Tony's boyhood memories was of his mother taking Papa to the emergency when he accidentally ate some."

"And…"

"Lorenza! Don't you think there is something very bizarre going on here? You didn't put favas in your filling. You even thought Emma had made a special mix. You said you wanted to taste what she'd done. And she didn't deny anything. She must have put the beans in his burrito. Emma must be close enough to the son to have known about his father's allergy. And to add icing to this gooey little story, it certainly interests me that Peters's secretary is the son's lover and must also have known Emma and was there the night Peters ate the favas. Maybe he brought the beans and slipped them to Emma on the back porch during one of her trips out for air. You never did find the burrito stuffing you didn't make, did you?"

"Did you ask this Antonio Petroni if he knew Emma?"

Lorenza was being infuriatingly stubborn about this one point. I sighed with pointed exasperation. "No. We only talked about his father. And he had to get back to work." I didn't want to tell her how I had upset him and that I had felt so guilty I had just let him talk about his father's death. I hadn't had the heart to bring up Emma after all.

"Maybe the names are a coincidence and he doesn't even know who Emma is."

I chewed the inside of my cheek to keep from screaming. "And the fava bean burrito filling?"

"We don't know what it was."

"Per Detective Thompson, favas are green when fresh…"

"I know what favas look like," she growled through clenched teeth. "Peters thought the filling had peas in it."

"All the better. If he thought the burrito was made of favas, he never would have eaten it and would have yelled bloody murder instead of being murdered!"

"Alice! Let me remind you that Emma is the one who nearly got murdered."

"Okay, so 'murder' is a little strong. Thompson said he died of a heart attack, possibly with a little help from an allergic reaction. Nothing certain. Maybe never certain. If I thought anyone had been trying to deliberately kill Peters, I wouldn't be talking to you about this. I'd have talked to Thompson. She's the professional. I just read mysteries for entertainment. I don't want to be one of those amateur sleuths, believe me."

"I hope not!"

"I just think someone was trying to make Peters sick for some reason or other. And with Peters, there must have been plenty of reasons."

"So why are you harping on this bizarre thing about Emma with some bean, which may have been something innocent like peas, and some men she may or may not know, and something she may or may not even have done? We don't know whether she actually prepared Peters's dinner either."

"Because…"

My phone rang just as I was supposed to explain my very convoluted theory to my very skeptical friend. For once I was grateful for telemarketers! Never again would I say they had no purpose other than to drive me insane or help the country slide further into never-ending commercialism. Never again would I be rude. I was so happy for the interruption, I was almost ready to buy, contribute, or participate in whatever intrusive survey they wanted. I gushed a hello.

It was not a telemarketer.

"For you, Lorenza. It's Thompson." I handed her the phone and watched as her expression went from neutral to astonished, from angry to confused. "What?" I asked when she hung up.

"Peters's son is threatening to sue me for gross negligence in serving favas to his father and contributing to his death."

Why was I not surprised?

CHAPTER 12

LIVORNO HAD NO attorney. It had never needed one before. Lawsuits just didn't happen here. But then no one had ever been accused of carelessly offing someone's father with favas, a bean with credentials as ancient as the famous blunt instrument, if one believed Pythagoras, at least. And that might depend on how you felt about him in geometry class.

Fortunately, Lorenza's major greengrocer, Carlo, had a brother who had a good friend who swore by a certain attorney with a practice in Berkeley. I didn't want to ask why this good friend of the brother of Carlo had so much business that he knew this attorney was that good. But Carlo is a nice guy, and I think he has a thing for Lorenza herself, not just her business, so I figured he wouldn't steer her wrong.

Unlike our Emma.

Well, that was still just my opinion. It wasn't that Lorenza didn't think I might have a point about the burrito filling being questionable. Nor did she disagree that the whole question of how favas popped up in Peters's fatal dinner might not need an answer. She just didn't think she should be harassing Emma about the matter until she was out of the hospital. I disagreed, of course. I thought a weakened Emma was more likely to tell the truth after a near brush with death. Probably got that out of some mystery novel, but the logic seemed perfectly good to me. But, for some reason as yet unclear to me, my good friend was fond of Emma.

Lorenza has an inordinately soft heart for injured creatures, crying children, starving raccoons…or any person who reminds her of them. And Lorenza is as loyal and protective as a fierce mother hen about those she takes under her wing. Growing up Catholic and of southern European immigrant stock in a WASP culture may have taught her, in an unmistakable way, how mindlessly cruel people can be to those they consider different, inferior, or weak. That experience may have been one reason she showed up on my doorstep the day after Frances died, with a pot of root vegetable soup in one hand, a box of tissues in the other, tears streaming down her cheeks, with full understanding of my grief.

At no time did she act as if Frances and I, who never pretended to have a relationship other than marital, were sinners or some kind of abnormal creatures. Lorenza once told me she'd never believe love could be deviant. Intolerance and hatred, yes. Love, never. Lorenza's God has always been a kind one. And if anyone was ever made in that God's image, it was definitely my friend.

Anyway, she was far more concerned about Emma's recovery and how the police investigation into the stabbing was going than she was about energetically pursuing answers on stuffings. Every time I brought up my concerns, Lorenza made it quite clear she thought I was putting far too much emphasis on the whole burrito thing. At some point, when they both had time, she said with an indifferent shrug, she'd talk to Elena about what had happened that night. In the meantime, the two were very busy working to reopen The Lovage.

Certainly she knew Emma better than I did, having interviewed her, checked references, and worked with her closely for several weeks prior to Peters's death. And she insisted Emma would give a perfectly good explanation when she was well enough to do so. Maybe she would. I just didn't think so.

But my suspicions about Emma's motives and the fava filling were causing some tension between Lorenza and me. I wasn't happy about that and opted to make peace. In the spirit of conciliation (and incidentally to reestablish my basic fairmindedness), I offered to bring Emma home from the hospital on the Saturday she was going to be released.

"Are you sure you want to do this?" Lorenza looked me directly in the eyes.

"Would I offer if I didn't?" I stared back just as intently.

"You won't take her on the scenic drive and drop her off a cliff?"

I shook my head in vigorous reassurance.

"You don't have to do this. I know you don't like her."

"I'm also sick of seeing you and Elena killing yourselves with work. The sooner Emma gets back, the better for the two of you. Hence, no cliff. I may just take each curve at 50 mph, however, and scare the living daylights out of her. After which, I'll grill her, if you'll pardon the expression, and make her promise to pay any damages from this lawsuit. Then I'll deliver her to you with her signed agreement never to serve anything unapproved by you again and chain her to the stove."

"Deliver her to me and not to Detective Thompson?"

"Why would I do that?" I didn't like the smile twitching at the corner of Lorenza's lips.

"I thought you rather fancied Thompson."

I coughed and tried to hide my face, which I knew to be turning a shade just to the left of beet. "She's married."

"To whom?"

"I rather lost track of that part of the conversation. I think I fainted in shock. Some male doctor or other, if I recall."

"My poor Alice! I'm sorry. I shouldn't tease you, but I did think you liked her and suspected she might return the feeling."

"I did like her...a bit." I smiled. Lorenza could be touchingly old-fashioned in her phrasing sometimes. "But I'm really rather glad nothing came of it. I prefer a comfortable friendship. It's much more fun."

"Hmm. I'm not sure I buy—"

"Meanwhile, I really don't mind picking Emma up. You and

Elena have enough to do. Since I've already cut your herbs, I've got the time to do it before I come over to the restaurant and help you with reservations and hostessing or whatever you can teach me quickly."

Lorenza raised her eyebrows. "You're not going to work at The Lovage on your days off!"

After all these years, I get a kick out of surprising her sometimes. "Actually, I thought I could probably get home early enough during the week most of the time to help until Emma's back again."

"You don't have to. Elena and I can manage."

"Could you use the extra help or not?"

"Of course, assuming anyone comes."

"They'll come. There's no question. The big question is whether I'm trainable or not."

"I'll pay you."

"Do something anatomically impossible to yourself, will you Lorenza? Pay me, and I won't work. No, wait. On second thought, you can feed me for free."

"You've gotten free dinners ever since The Lovage opened."

"Then put that in my employment contract. By the way, you're my next of kin. If nothing else, I know you know your own phone number and address in case something happens to me."

"Thanks for the vote of confidence in the memory department, but please don't get yourself stabbed like Emma. Promise?"

"No reason I should. Anyway, I better get going if I'm to get home in time for my training."

"You're a good woman, Alice."

"Bleep you."

"Hurry back. You're on company time."

CHAPTER 13

THE SIGHT OF wan Emma waiting for me in a wheelchair at the hospital emergency entrance was enough to make me think Lorenza might be right about her head chef after all. At this particular moment, anyway, she certainly didn't look like anyone capable of anything more serious than simple culinary stupidity.

Peters was the dead one, however, not Emma Stilwell. But to be fair (and I was practicing this for Lorenza's sake), even I couldn't really imagine her wanting to do anything worse than make him sick. First of all, favas are hardly as efficient as guns, knives, or even poison if murder had been her purpose. Second, I doubted that cold-blooded killers ever looked like Emma. But what do I know? The only actual murderers I've seen are in post office mug shots or news photos of the suspects being taken to trial. The former confirm general public opinion that anyone wanted for a crime is a wild-eyed lunatic. The latter are so cleaned up anyone would think the defendants were just your average Joe/Josephine in a jumpsuit. Both are about as phony as you can get.

So I suppose Peters's death could have been a deliberate plan for petty revenge that went tragically wrong. Emma did have a failed restaurant in her past. Had a bad review from Peters done her in? On the other hand the whole thing might really have been an unfortunate culinary experiment with unforeseen results, as Lorenza was inclined to think.

Which did I honestly think happened: that it was an innocent mistake or that Emma was instrumental in getting those favas into the burrito with deliberate and malicious intent? The latter. Favas are just too bizarre a thing to slip into a burrito not to have been put there with malice aforethought, so to speak. No matter how I looked at it, unless the whole fava business was, in fact, just pure stupidity and bad luck, Emma was legally guilty of something, even if death was not the intent.

Then there was that other question: Did the police care? Probably not. Even if they were concerned, the police were putting all of the few resources they had into finding who had stabbed Emma. Favas were just a petty bickering factor in a lawsuit over the death of a man with a serious heart condition who had died, most significantly, from a heart attack just waiting to happen. Somehow, I did not think Detective Thompson would really want to make time in her busy day just to listen to some theory from me about Emma and lethal beans.

Anyway, Emma was paler than the white-clad aide standing behind her wheelchair. Gone were the roses under cream-colored skin. She had that blue cast skim milk used to have before the dairy industry realized people liked blue milk even less than Bush liked broccoli.

As soon as she was safely in the car, I reached over and turned on the heat. Although it was technically the summer season, it was one of those northern California summer days that would qualify as autumn anywhere else.

"Are you sure you feel well enough to be going home?" I asked.

She shivered slightly, then looked away as if embarrassed by her show of weakness.

Had I liked Emma more, I would have let her save face. Instead, I said, "Wait a minute. I'll get the blanket from the trunk."

But hurt pride or no, when I draped the dark green, soft-weave cotton blanket around her shoulders, over her arms, and into her lap, she looked up at me and smiled. That smile was the strongest thing about an otherwise fragile-looking person.

"Thank you," she said. "Actually, I'd rather go home than stay here no matter what the doctor said. I'll feel better just sleeping in my own bed." Her voice came in for the second strongest.

"I can understand that. But I'd have to have Edward and Piers too."

"Edward and Piers?"

"My cats."

"Of course. I remember you talking about them! They're pretty special little guys, after all." The way she smiled would have made Lorenza realize she had another cat nut on her hands had she been there to see it. For just an instant, I genuinely warmed to Emma.

After that, however, she looked so tired I decided to let her talk only if she wanted. For a while I thought she had fallen asleep, until halfway home when I looked over and saw her staring out the window at the cattle grazing on the dry hay-colored hills.

"Lorenza didn't call anyone about what happened," I said. "Did you want me to call a friend or family member? Someone to come stay with you for a few days?" I was actually fishing, very subtly as usual, for some specific information.

"No. I can take care of myself," she said in a sharp tone of voice. Then she looked at me a little sheepishly. "Sorry. I meant except for your kindness in getting me home, that is. But it's okay. Really. I'll be all right by myself."

I'm a little stubborn—on rare occasions. "I'm not so sure about that," I said in a voice I hoped would quell any argument. "You could probably use someone with you for a bit."

"Maybe you could loan me a cat?"

That was certainly a clever distraction. Emma was smarter than I had given her credit for. But I had time, so I decided to pretend I was a hooked fish and run with her line for a while.

"It would have to be both or neither. They're an inseparable pair. Neither goes anywhere without the other, even if only one has to go to the vet. I'd gladly loan you both, but I don't think you're up to the nine o'clock crazies from two very vocal felines. Underneath those cute gray-striped fur coats lie the souls of two Tasmanian Devils."

"You gave them interesting names. Why 'Edward' and 'Piers'?"

"Edward II of England and Piers Gaviston, his lover." I gave her a quick sideglance, an automatic thing with heterosexuals I didn't know, to see how she took the concept. Of course, if she was close to Tony Petroni she must have been comfortable with his relationship with John. On the other hand, not necessarily. To her credit, she didn't do the usual nervous blink and eye-slide routine.

"My history's shaky. Don't tell me yet…" She hesitated just a moment. "A Plantagenet. Yes? Can't remember…oh, maybe 1400s?"

Yet another surprise about Emma. She'd actually read something besides *Woman's Home Weekly* and *The Cook's Companion*.

"Close enough. Early 1300s. Great grandson to King John."

"John. Not a nice man, if I remember. Presumably Edward was better, or you wouldn't have named your cat after him." Emma smiled.

There was an unusually gentle quality to her voice. It reminded me of the night Peters died and she had shown such tenderness to Lorenza. This woman was clearly showing more facets than I had given her credit for, and now I wasn't sure what direction I wanted to take with my queries. What kind of person was I dealing with here? For want of a clever response and to give myself time to regroup, I just answered her question.

"Who knows? Edward II has never gotten good press. But consider who wrote the history: a bunch of antigay bigots."

I checked for a reaction. There wasn't one. Emma seemed to be listening, albeit with a slight frown. Was it from irritation—or just from the effort of concentrating? I blithered onward.

"He and Piers were absolutely devoted to each other, but they didn't try to hide their relationship. I won't say they were perfect and they didn't make stupid mistakes. Without doubt, Piers was arrogant and Edward wouldn't compromise. But weaker kings have been tolerated—or at least for far longer." I thumped the steering wheel for emphasis. "What destroyed them was their lack of hypocrisy and the fears of the ignorant."

I could hear myself gearing up for what Frances used to call my Free Lectures to the Uninformed. I could almost feel her cautionary nudge to shut up. But I do so love a good rant when I have a captive, if not necessarily receptive, audience.

"In a world where male military comradeship was critical to survival," I continued with great relish, "homosexuality was a major fear. And people seem to want to destroy either what they fear or what symbolizes their fears. The openness of the relationship between Edward and Piers scared them. So the fine Christians of the time sawed Piers's head off and put a hot poker up Edward's rear. I don't think the symbolism of the poker bit was lost on anyone."

Emma shuddered. "Grisly."

"Anyway, when Frances and I got the kittens, they were so devoted to each other, we decided to name them after those two. Give Edward and Piers a second chance to have a peaceful and happy life under better circumstances, in a manner of speaking."

"A sort of reincarnation?"

"Symbolically. Wouldn't it be nice if those more sinned against than sinning could have second chances like that?" I was warming to my subject. When I got into one of these preachy moods, Frances used to ask whether the McDoughalls were direct descendants of some ministerial coven.

"Of course. But do you really think Edward and Piers were so perceptive? I'd find it a real stretch to imagine those guys so secure in the decency of their love for each other that they'd flaunt the conventions of their world quite so courageously. For the most part, people are creatures of what they've been told, and I thought everyone in those days believed 'sodomites' went to hell?"

And Frances never argued with me. Maybe she had enough sense not to. Emma clearly didn't.

I hesitated. The road was winding down gently into a sparsely wooded area in a small valley. Just ahead of us was a small lake at the curve of highway. The weak sunlight reflected in fiery flashes from the wind-rippled water.

"Remember the theory that the earth, not the sun, was the center of the solar system?"

She nodded.

"Not only was that conventional wisdom for ages, but it was heresy to think otherwise. A few were even burned at the stake for saying differently. Yet even then, some knew the earth wasn't the center."

I glanced over at Emma. She was looking at me, but her expression was unreadable.

"So I see no reason not to conclude that Edward and Piers were more enlightened than others of their time. Maybe there really isn't any evidence to prove that. Maybe the documentation was destroyed. Or maybe no one wants to search out the evidence because our society still thinks there is something horrible about being gay."

"Okay, I see your point. And I think you'd say how sad it was that people were burned for being right."

"Of course."

"But isn't it just as tragic that there are those so paralyzed by fear of another way of being or thinking that they brutally slaughter other humans in order to silence them? Creatures with the same basic look, feelings, and social habits as the murderers? These weren't foreign creatures like insects, reptiles, or even animals killed for food. They were a mirror image of the person with the torch."

My mouth was opened for a roar of protest. Then I bit my tongue. Emma's voice was hoarse and weak. Fighting her could wait until she was well and a worthy adversary.

"I'm sorry. Frances used to say I should carry a soapbox with me on all occasions just in case of need." I smiled, pretty sincerely suggesting a truce.

Emma turned her head and was staring at the parched and empty straw-covered hills. We'd passed the cows.

"Frances was your lover."

"You know Plato's *Symposium?* Frances was my missing half. She was the companion of my dreams who was always there even when I woke up from them. She's dead."

Emma slipped on her dark glasses before she looked at me. I couldn't see her eyes, only black circles above an expressionless mouth.

"Lorenza told me."

I was instantly annoyed with Lorenza. What business had she to tell this total stranger about my private life? I ignored the little voice of reason hiding behind my better self and continued. "She was a painter, a very gifted one, I thought. She was killed stupidly, uselessly, because some fool thought he could drive drunk and none of his friends had the guts to stop him."

"I'm sorry, Alice." Emma turned her head as far from me as possible. I didn't know whether she was sympathizing with my loss or apologizing for her compassion pitch for the ignorant who kill. But I did know from her voice that she was crying.

My sense of reason began to scream at me for attention. This time I listened. Frances would have been proud of me.

"I'm the one who should be sorry," I said. "Let's change the subject. You don't need to hear all this from me right now."

She took off her glasses and quickly ran her hand under her eyes. "Okay. But sometime I would like to hear about Frances."

That even sounded genuine. I was beginning to have very mixed feelings about Emma. For both our sakes, it was time for a safe subject.

"By the way, Lorenza made you some of her split pea soup for dinner. It has parsnips." I waited a minute, then looked at Emma. She was smiling at me.

"Lorenza is a sweetheart. She's been incredibly kind and certainly doesn't deserve this business with Peters and, to top it all off, have an out-of-commission chef. Even with Elena, she's got too much to do. Hopefully, I'll be able to get back to work in a few days."

Looking at her, I doubted that. On the other hand, this feigned innocence annoyed me, and I shoved my newly generous self into the background again. "I'm filling in when I can, but I wish the Peters thing really had ended with his death. This other is just too much."

Never let it be said that I'm less tenacious than a dog with a bone. Her wounds aside, I had not forgotten how pissed I was that Emma's friend and Peters's son was suing Lorenza. Seeing Tony with John rather put paid to the idea of Emma and Tony being lovers in the manner of Bonnie and Clyde, but I still felt there was something nefarious going on.

"What other thing?"

I glared at her as ferociously as I could and still keep my eyes on the road. She had the unmitigated gall to look perplexed. In fact, quite genuinely perplexed. I didn't buy the innocent pose for a second.

"Lorenza being sued by Peters's son, of course. Antonio Petroni? You know. Tony?" I snarled.

"That's impossible."

Well, give her one point for audacity but then whip her once for it too. "The hell it is!" I said.

"Alice, I know it is. Tony is a good friend of mine. He'd never sue Lorenza just because his father had a heart attack in her restaurant."

And another point for acknowledging she knew Peters Junior. But take it away for pretending not to know the basis for the suit. "It wasn't just a heart attack, as you well know."

Emma's cheeks flushed an angry red. Considering her weakened state, that was pretty impressive. Either she was outraged at the accusation because she was innocent, or she was a damned good actor. For five hot seconds I was willing to give her the benefit of the doubt. I was trying desperately for points in the Being Fair category.

"What do you mean by 'as you well know'? I certainly do not."

She'd had her moment of mercy.

"He apparently had a severe allergic reaction to some fava beans that had found their way, rather inexplicably, into the burrito he ate. The shock was too much for his heart. And he did have a weakened heart, you know. Your friend Tony is claiming Lorenza is guilty of gross negligence." What that statement may have lacked in strict forensic veracity, it more than made up for in good dramatic punch.

Fortunately, I suppose, Emma is a young woman. At the rate her skin color was changing from red to white and back again, Tony might have had grounds for another suit. This one against me for shocking his friend into a stroke.

I chewed on my tongue to keep from saying anything else. Emma said nothing and turned her head away. We drove on in an utter but very palpable silence.

"Are you sure the favas were in the burrito?" Emma's voice was so controlled it was monotone.

"They couldn't have been in the salad. He only ate one leaf of that. I watched him."

"But we thought Lorenza had brought that burrito filling."

I pounded the steering wheel. My anger on Lorenza's behalf just overflowed the dam. "She has never put favas into a burrito filling! That's number one. Number two, she knows they can make some men sick and would have made sure the menu clearly listed favas as an ingredient if she had used them."

More silence. I tried to regain my calm. Sanity while driving is usually a good idea.

Then something Emma had just said registered. "What do you mean Lorenza brought *that* burrito filling?"

"The filling in the large earthenware bowl. It was on the countertop next to the box of vegetables. Elena picked it up and used it for the burrito orders. We thought Lorenza had brought it."

I remembered the large bowl. I had carried it in from the porch. "I brought that bowl in," I said. "It was sitting next to the pots of salad nasturtiums on the landing outside the kitchen." And I had thought it was something Lorenza had prepared too.

"Oh."

Indeed! "What happened to it? Remember? You couldn't find it later."

"I know. I lied about that. I tossed it, Alice. Elena had used it for Peters's burrito. Neither of us thought it was one of Lorenza's usual recipes, but she had told Elena and me she was going to make a special filling at home to save us all time. The stuff in the earthenware bowl was labeled "burrito filling" and was right next to the vegetables and herbs you brought. Maybe we should have asked, but with a short staff and Lorenza overseeing the Peters party, everything was crazy, and we just assumed it was what it looked like. Later on, we found some more in the refrigerator. That mix looked different. When I found out Peters had keeled over, I panicked. I didn't want…well, I didn't want any problems for either Elena or Lorenza, so I threw the whole thing from the earthenware bowl in the Dumpster."

"But we didn't know why he had died at that point. What made you think there was a problem with the stuff in the bowl?"

She hesitated. "I can't explain. As I said, I just panicked. Panic isn't logical, and you know I wasn't myself that night."

And how should I know, I thought. On the other hand, Lorenza would certainly agree that Emma wasn't herself. Maybe I should check with Lorenza and Elena and get their side of the story. Could Emma be telling the truth? If so, where did the bowl come from and who brought it? The number of potential suspects suddenly grew infinite.

Well, not quite. There was still the lawsuit, and I still suspected Emma of hiding something. After all, when the three of us were sitting in the kitchen that night, Lorenza made it clear she thought Emma had made the filling. Why didn't Emma come clean then, when she found out the mix wasn't something Lorenza had prepared?

The car crested the hill just before the descent into Livorno, and the view pleasantly distracted me from my thoughts. From this angle, the town looked like a small, Mediterranean-style cliff dwelling. The multicolored houses, fringed with vivid gardens and separated by narrow and impossibly steep little black streets, were tightly packed against the hillside above the small cove off the ocean. The image made me think of a quilt, draped over the cliffs, with borders resting on the edge of the old brown wharves.

I loved this town. It was worth the hellish commute to San Francisco. One of these days, I would retire and never leave my garden, or at least go no farther than The Lovage.

"Alice?"

I started, reluctantly pulling myself back from my pleasurable little reverie, which definitely included neither Emma Stilwell nor Arthur Peters. "Yes," I snapped.

"This is going to sound odd."

As if nothing has so far?

"You're being unbelievably kind to take me home."

Don't take it personally, I thought. I'm doing this for Lorenza.

"But may I ask another favor of you?"

I nodded an affirmation. I was willing to run to the grocery store for her or similar. I had promised I would.

"Could we stop by your house? I really want to meet your cats before I go back to my apartment."

I blinked twice, swallowed once, and nodded. "Sure," I said. "Why not?"

They'll probably hide under the bed anyway.

CHAPTER 14

THE PETRONI *VS.* Galli lawsuit did hit the papers. Fortunately, the article was short on specifics and was on the fourth page of the food section in a column of miscellaneous restaurant news. Local celebrity or not, Peters had been bumped by a really bad day on the stock market. Jittery investing boomers care more about interviews with experts on the bulls and the bears than any article about a lawsuit over food allergies when the Dow goes diving. And from Peters's point of view, he might have preferred being next to an article on the joys of radishes; food was his thing after all.

In any event, the first Sunday at The Lovage was light, but customers were coming back. The regulars thumped Lorenza sympathetically on the back and, with a slightly self-conscious resolve, marched to their usual tables. The curious, those who just wanted to tell their friends they had actually eaten where-it-had-all-happened, came as expected. I doubted many of them would ever come back, but I hoped I was wrong.

It was the genuinely new business that stayed away, and Lorenza worried. I didn't blame her. I would have felt better myself if the whole incident had ended with Peters's death too. But thanks to fava beans and Peters Junior, it hadn't. It was almost as if Peters was determined to finish Lorenza off from the grave. And I wouldn't have put it past him either.

As Joan had said, people have died of heart attacks in restaurants before with no ill effect on business. But I was concerned about the long-term effects of the lawsuit. It was sure to be dragged out as these things always are. The law is slow; justice is even slower.

By the second week, however, telephone reservations, at least for the weekend, had picked up, and I saw new customers who seemed more intent on reading the menu than looking around, pointing, and whispering.

"Told you so!" I crowed ever so slightly to Lorenza and Elena one night into the third week. We were sitting in the kitchen after closing. Lorenza and Elena were sharing a bottle of Negro Modelo and I was into my second glass of white Burgundy.

Elena nodded at me and said to Lorenza, "Our little friend is always so modest!" Elena delighted in teasing me because I towered a good half foot over her sixty-inch self. She never teased Lorenza, however, who was a little sensitive about her own height.

"And too quick to judge. The weather's been hot. Too hot to cook at home. That's why business picked up. Just wait." Lorenza was grouchy from both the heat and fatigue.

"Is that why most of the new reservations were from San Francisco and Marin County? It's too hot to cook, but they'll drive all the way out here on a hot evening to come for dinner? Wouldn't dream of coming back, of course."

"So maybe you and Emma have a point." Lorenza's concession to evidence was too grudging. I suspected she just wanted me to shut up so she could sweat in peace.

"And how is Emma?" Elena asked Lorenza.

"I talked to her last night. Her doctor cleared her to come back part-time next week."

Emma had not yet returned to work. There were complications with the wound healing and an infection had set in. I had taken her back and forth to the hospital a couple of times. And despite wanting to ask her more questions about the events on the night of Peters's death, even I didn't have the heart to press her. She was not a well woman.

On the other hand, I now had both Elena and Lorenza together, perhaps mellow with good ale and even willing to talk.

"By the way, I'm curious about something Emma mentioned the first time I brought her home from the hospital."

"Yes, little one?"

"The burrito filling you used for Peters's dinner. Where did it come from?"

"It was in a bowl by the box of vegetables. We assumed Lorenza brought it from home."

"What bowl?" Lorenza's eyebrows shot up. "We had a box of herbs and one of vegetables. I made my filling early that morning and put it in the refrigerator. I thought you were using that."

"We're talking about the earthenware one sitting on the landing outside the kitchen," I said. "I assumed you had put it down to open the door and forgotten to take it inside."

"I don't remember any earthenware bowl, and I certainly didn't bring it."

Interesting. "I carried it inside and left it by the box."

"And I used it for the burrito filling." Elena got up, grabbed another Negro Modelo from her secret private cache, and poured another half glass, passing the rest of the bottle to Lorenza. That was half a glass more than Elena usually had after work. She had to be pretty worn out.

"What did the mix look like?" I asked.

"Green and brown. Like mint ice cream and milk chocolate." Elena winked mischievously at me.

I smiled. That certainly sounded better than green peas in brown library paste.

"But I never made that." Lorenza looked a little gray in the cheeks and gulped half her ale.

"Emma was curious about the mix when she saw me making a burrito with it. She asked if it was the special filling you were going to make. It didn't look like anything you'd ever done before. But it was just too crazy in the kitchen, and I think we all just forgot about it."

"How many dinners did you fix with that stuff?" Lorenza asked.

"Four or five. None was sent back. Two went to the Peters party. Then we found the other bowl in the refrigerator. That looked like your usual. I tasted both. The one from the first bowl was spicier, but it made sense to Emma and me that Peters would get something a little unusual."

Nobody spoke for a moment. We just sat and stared at each other.

"I think we have a problem," I said finally.

"Where did it come from if you didn't make it?" Elena asked Lorenza.

"Maybe Emma knows?" Lorenza's voice had a hopeful tone.

"She obviously told Elena that night she thought you had made it, and she told me the same thing later," I said. "So she either doesn't know or she's a good actor."

"And when did you ask her this, did you say?" My good friend was rubbing her eyes.

"Relax, Lorenza. I asked her the first time I brought her home from the hospital. I thought she should know about the lawsuit. I didn't grill." Much.

Lorenza just shook her head at me. "But didn't we look for it that night? We never found the filling."

"The last time I used it was the last time I saw the bowl."

"Emma also told me she tossed it after she heard Peters was probably dead." And if that information didn't introduce a healthy little credibility issue to their minds I didn't know what would.

"Why?" they both asked in unison.

Very good!

"She panicked, she said. She didn't really give me a reason." Surely the gap was now widening.

"Well, she certainly wasn't herself that night," sang the chorus.

If the two of them didn't stop saying the same thing, I'd have to redefine the term twin set.

"Someone definitely threw it into the Dumpster, so I assume Emma told me the truth. I saw it there while I was waiting for the police and ambulance after she got stabbed."

"Poor darling! I think she was trying to protect us." Elena looked sadly at Lorenza. "She thought you made the filling, and she knew I had used it for Peters's burrito."

So much for the credibility gap.

"So, where did the bowl come from?" I pushed. If Emma was trying to protect the two of them, she certainly knew more about Peters's fava sensitivity than she was admitting.

"Someone on the staff must have made it. For themselves, maybe. Probably didn't realize we might use it by accident. I'd guess they meant to take it home later and forgot in all the excitement."

"That lovely theory, Lorenza, holds about as much water as a sieve. Surely someone would have realized they had forgotten their culinary masterpiece and said something, at least before the basis of the lawsuit hit the news?"

"I'll ask around." Lorenza looked like she was making a serious study of the ale left in the bottom of her bottle.

The Lovage hardly has a huge staff, either, I thought. I began counting them on my two hands and ended up with the toes.

"Any progress on who might have stabbed Emma?," Elena asked.

"I haven't heard anything. Poor thing. She's been through so much!"

"True," I conceded, then turned to Elena. "You know I thought you were annoyed with Emma the night Peters died. Like maybe she wasn't pulling her weight?"

Lorenza gave me a weary glare but didn't say anything.

"I was." Elena frowned as she thought about my question. "It was so unusual for her. She normally came early, had everything organized, and worked like a dog. She was a great chef, always open to new ideas and fun to work with. That night she was late, disorganized, and…distracted, I guess I'd say. After she made a mess of the salad dressing, she couldn't seem to do anything right, kept dropping things, and was more in the way than a help. When she finally disappeared out back, I was almost grateful."

I remembered Emma sobbing on the back landing. A little more than distracted, I'd say. "Did anyone ever ask why she came back to the restaurant later that night?"

"She told Detective Thompson she couldn't remember if anyone had locked up. Same reason you had. Why?" Lorenza asked.

"Just curious." And how odd, I thought. Emma had driven off before either Lorenza or I had walked out the door. Maybe I had reason to wonder if Lorenza had forgotten to lock the building because I was there, couldn't remember, and knew I hadn't. But why would Emma, already disorganized and distracted by god-knows-what personal problem, assume at least one of us wouldn't have done what we always did?

I glanced up at my two friends, expecting to see the same curiosity I was feeling reflected in their eyes. Instead, Lorenza had picked up the food section of the local paper, and Elena was getting up to toss the empty Negro Modelo bottles.

To say I was annoyed was to put it mildly. "So you don't know what was wrong with Emma that night?" If the locking-up issue was too subtle for them to worry about, perhaps this more obvious question about the night of Peters's death would grab their attention.

Lorenza didn't even glance up from the recipe she was reading. "Nerves," she said.

"Probably." Elena punctuated her confirmation by tossing the bottles into the recycle bin.

"And I'll talk to her about it when she is well enough to come back to work." Lorenza turned the page very carefully and quite purposely did not look in my direction.

What was it going to take to instill a little healthy suspicion in either of these two?

CHAPTER 15

I GAVE UP trying to talk to Lorenza about how distrustful I was about Emma and her possible involvement with the favas. Even Elena joined my good friend in her new mantra: "O-poor-pitiful-suffering-Emma." It got so bad, I began to feel I was abusing the woman when I even thought that all was not so innocent with the new chef. I alternated between feeling like the wicked witch of the west and knowing I wasn't completely crazy to think the leaps of faith Emma had expected us all to make with her story, or lack thereof, were just a tad long.

But even my cats had joined the Emma fan club. Now, there, I felt really betrayed.

THE DAY EMMA had asked to see Edward and Piers, I had agreed, with the unspoken and blithe assumption that they would do their usual thing and be utterly inhospitable.

Of the two, Piers is the more gracious host—but not on the first meeting. On the first visit he peers around the corner at the intruder (aka my guest) and then flies away down the hall at warp speed should the poor soul attempt to be friendly. I have had to replace the hall carpet twice because his claws have left more divots than Tiger Woods could even imagine.

Edward, on the other hand, has the manners of Hagar the Horrible. He is, shall we say, slightly paranoid. He even runs from Lorenza on occasion. And, if I really believed he was the reincarnation of his namesake, I'd understand why he didn't trust anyone.

"You'll be lucky to see the tips of their tails," I had warned as Emma and I got to my house that day. "Especially Edward. He's probably already under the bed."

Nope.

The minute Emma walked into the living room, Edward stopped in mid-flee, came back, studied her for a full minute, and jumped into her lap as soon as she sat down. He even purred. The little brat actually took to the woman. If I hadn't known better, I'd have sworn they were mother and son reunited after years of separation.

"Isn't Stilwell an Anglo-Saxon name?" I muttered, staring at Edward as if he really had been a Plantagenet over six hundred years ago.

"What?" Emma was cheerfully petting the traitor.

"Nothing. Just talking to myself. Like some tea?"

BUT EDWARD IS not stupid. Quirky, yes. Stupid, no. Consequently, I took his acceptance of Emma with some seriousness. Cat people will understand this. Actually, dog people will too. Don't we all trust our pet's instincts about people? Okay, so I do.

Therefore, shortly after the little discussion with Lorenza and Elena, I decided it was time to have a wee talk with Edward. As soon as I got home from work and had fed the three of us, I went into the living room and patted the space beside me on the sofa.

"Edward?"

He was sitting in the middle of the room, washing himself after an acceptable dinner of crab in aspic, albeit canned and labeled for cats only. He briefly stopped, looked up at me, and finished his face in his own good time. Then he stretched, yawned, and walked over to me at a pace leisurely enough to remind me that little demands haste in this world, despite what humans may think.

I patted the sofa again. He decided my lap was more appealing and leapt into it. Fortunately, I was not wearing pantyhose. He definitely needed his claws clipped.

Curling into a fur circle and commencing to purr, he became

the complete picture of innocence in feline form. "Oh, you're so cute," I caught myself saying. And, of course, he knew it.

"Edward, I know you took to Emma."

The volume of his purr turned up a notch.

"But there is something I don't trust about her."

The circle of fur tightened protectively.

"I'm not saying she doesn't have her good points."

He licked his nose and looked up at me. Now what in the hell did that mean?

"I guess I think I really, sort of, maybe, in a strange way, find her likable—at least interesting—too. But like her or not, she is hiding something. And something odd was going on the night Peters died. And she's involved somehow. I just know it. Not being herself does not explain why she threw out the burrito mix when she heard Peters had died. She had absolutely no good reason to think there was a connection unless she knew that favas were in that mix and Peters was allergic to them. Lorenza and Elena may buy into her story that she reacted precipitously because she just wasn't herself, but I don't. And frankly, if she hadn't been stabbed that night, maybe I could generate a little more interest in this theory."

Edward stretched out one back leg, shook it, and immediately pulled it back underneath himself. This was far too subtle a commentary for my simple mind as well.

"Did she bring the mix herself? But, if she did, why did she let Elena fix Peters's burrito and several others and then throw it out, almost as if she wanted to protect Elena? Did someone bring it for her to fix for Peters? But, again, why let Elena do the prep unless she was trying to punt the blame, which still doesn't explain why she threw it out later. And why not throw it out after Peters got his food? Could she really be totally innocent, and did someone plant it for her to find and use? Did she genuinely think it was Lorenza's recipe?"

Edward chose that moment to sneeze all over my hand.

"Thanks for the editorial opinion!"

Unfortunately, I'm neither Miss Marple nor V. I. Warshawski. On the other hand, I'm paid to think at my job. Maybe the skills were transferable to real life. I petted the soft, warm cat body in my lap and tried to work out something logical, but these circumstances were not going to fit easily into the bullet-format talking points for mid-level executives at high-level planning sessions, not that those do either, but that's something else.

"Anyone in that dining room could have brought the fava mix. Anyone in Northern California could have. In fact, someone in Maine, who hated Peters, could have had them flown in specially and delivered…Oh, hell!"

Edward began to snore. These may have seemed possibilities to me, but they were obviously both boring and irrelevant to him.

"Okay, so answers are usually simpler than that. The most obvious person to want to harm Peters, for whatever reason, is someone close to him. At Walton Square, Tony told me that he is an only child. He also said that he and his father had been estranged for quite a few years and only recently made peace. Why were they estranged, and did they really make up? He also said that his mother, Peters's ex-wife, is dead, so she's out of the suspect pool. There is no conceivable reason why Peters's current girlfriend would want him anything but healthy, wealthy, and able to write checks for her credit card bills. And then there is John, who has just a 'wee bit of temper.' I would more likely suspect him of bludgeoning someone to death, but who knows? Maybe he is capable of greater subtlety than I saw that day? And then there is John's weekly heterosexual date. Maybe she got tired of the game and decided she wanted to make Peters feel as sick as she did of the scam with John. And then there is the possibility that someone whose livelihood had been destroyed by a bad review would want to play a rather crude joke on Peters, not realizing it could be a fatal one."

Edward stopped snoring, opened one eye, and looked at me.

"I wonder what happened to Emma's restaurant? Why did it fail, and did Peters have anything to do with it?"

Edward was now giving me his undivided attention.

"You know, I really think the fava business was a bad practical joke gone wrong. I don't think whoever came up with the idea actually meant to kill Peters. After all, Pythagoras aside, favas are not the most efficient blunt instrument in criminal history. Maybe Tony wanted to teach his father a lesson about something and got Emma to go along with it? Maybe the girlfriend wanted to scare him into marriage? Maybe John wanted a raise and figured Peters wouldn't be so cheap if he got sick and scared? And all of this sounds too much like a soap opera."

That got a big yawn. Edward isn't into the soaps. Actually, he isn't into TV, unless it's a rerun of Glenda Jackson playing Elizabeth I.

"And maybe Emma went along because she had some history with Peters. But, if so, why was she so upset when she heard Tony was suing? He hadn't told her about that part? She wasn't getting a cut and she wanted it? Okay, so that is a little mean. As much as I hate to admit this, I really don't think Emma knew about the lawsuit. But I feel even more strongly that she knows more than she's admitting about the favas and where they came from."

A very loud purr from Edward.

"But then there is the problem of getting the favas into Peters's stomach. He wouldn't even have known the burrito was on the menu unless someone had slipped him a list of dishes for the night, and, even then, there was still no guarantee he would choose that particular item. Sure, I figured he would, half in jest, but he could have chosen almost anything else just as easily."

Edward had gone back to sleep.

"And then there is this lawsuit? Is that part of the plan or incidental? Lorenza is not a wealthy woman. There is not a lot of money to be gotten out of this. And frankly, I don't see Tony as the type to sue. Actually, I don't even see John doing it. I still see him as your classic hatchet man. Mind you, I really don't know either of them well."

I think the cat snorted.

"And Lorenza doesn't have any enemies. She has no real competitors in Livorno, and I honestly can't think of anyone who'd want to do her in. I'd like to choke her sometimes for having more heart than greed, but that's different. There is her driving, but…"

Edward began to twitch. I wondered if the prey in his dream was as illusive as the prey I was trying to imagine.

"Damn it! Emma's guilty of something. I don't think anyone is out for Lorenza—unless it's Emma. Could she be trying to get Lorenza out of business so she can buy the restaurant at rock-bottom prices and get back into business herself with The Lovage?"

Edward was now making eating noises in his sleep. Apparently, he had caught what he was chasing. At least Edward's prey was edible. The image of Emma on a platter with an apple in her mouth suddenly popped into my mind.

I sat silently for a few minutes.

"You know, that stabbing is a little strange too. Not that it couldn't happen here, but people in Livorno still leave their doors unlocked. Even I don't lock my garage and I grew up in San Francisco. The Lovage is on the main street. That's well lighted. The back isn't, but there are houses behind the restaurant, so breaking and entering is pretty risky. And anyone who knows Lorenza's habits knows she doesn't leave money around, except in the safe. If someone was trying to break into the building, he either hadn't done his homework or was pretty stupid. And, if Emma had interrupted him—or—them trying to break in, why not just bop her on the head and run? What was with the knife?"

Edward sat up, stretched in that statuelike position cats do, and yawned. He was clearly getting bored with my snailish, typically human speed of thought.

"So could Emma be trying to hide something or someone that might have led to the attack on her? Maybe I really did save her life! On the other hand, why would someone, trying to do her injury, know she was even going to be down there? Oh, Edward, this is getting to be too much for me to figure out. I think it is all too complicated. Besides, I'm sure Detective Thompson is doing a fine job trying to catch Emma's assailant."

I smiled at the thought of the detective.

Edward did not. If a cat could glare, he did.

"What do you expect me to do? I have neither the intention nor the interest in getting involved with who stabbed Emma. I'm quite happy to leave that whole mess to the professionals." I hesitated. "On the other hand, no one seems that concerned about any connection between the lawsuit and Emma's strange behavior with the fava mix—mainly because she was stabbed. Now a lawsuit—that's something I can get my teeth into!"

Edward was looking at me with great concentration.

"Thompson is not the person to talk to on this. She's far too busy, and, besides, she'd think I was silly. I also don't trust my motives in talking to her. I like her a bit too much, and she's straight." At least I didn't feel embarrassed confessing that to the cat.

Edward continued to stare at me with immense patience. I had just fed him, so I assumed he didn't want dinner. I decided he wanted me to go on with my thoughts.

"I could call Emma and talk to her, I suppose."

Edward put his paw on my mouth.

"I really didn't want to do that anyway," I said through his foot. "She wasn't all that forthcoming, and she really has been through a lot. Lorenza would probably get a restraining order against me if I persisted in what she'd view as harassment anyway."

The cat jumped off my lap and sat facing me.

"There is Tony, who either is or is not involved in whatever is going on...or not going on. Somehow I can't imagine he's guilty of anything. No man who's mature enough to live with his bald spot exposed and cry in front of a stranger could be all that bad. Of course, there is dear John, who, if he isn't involved in this mess, should be a suspect in something, with that temper of his."

The proverbial light was beginning to flash.

"And if Tony is as innocent as I suspect he is, then maybe, just maybe, he could be talked out of this lawsuit. Maybe, too, he could shed some light on his good friend, Emma, maybe his beloved John, or even enough about his father to give me some insight. He seemed willing enough to talk to me the other day. Maybe naïve directness would have just the right touch. After all, I'm just a silly old biddy with no understanding of the complicated world of lawsuit do's and don'ts. Maybe I really should call Tony."

Breathless after such a Jamesian period of extended hard thought, I looked at Edward, still sitting squarely in front of me. "Now," I said, "what do you think of *that?*"

Edward stood, arched his back in a good stretch, and walked away. But I would have sworn that cat winked at me in reply.

CHAPTER 16

I CAN'T REMEMBER how often I've heard people say that San Francisco is a city without seasons. Wrong. San Francisco has an infinite variety of seasons. They change daily. They vary from district to district on any given day, and sometimes they change at any time on any given day in any particular place. Growing up, I remember mornings when I'd wake up in winter, have recess at school in spring, lunch in summer, and go home in an autumn afternoon. Just to complicate things further, seasons in the city bear minimal resemblance to what is going on in the rest of the Bay Area.

Thus it had been summer all day in Livorno, which lies several miles to the north of the city. Now, at six P.M., it was winter on Duncan Street.

Upper Duncan sits above Noe Valley on the edge of Diamond Heights. Gardens are naturally lush here, fuchsias really do grow wild, and the views are spectacular. So are the gigantic billows of fog, which cascade down Twin Peaks in July pushed by whipping winds. People in the East Bay or even the Mission are planning warm, sunny barbecues for the long weekend while people on Duncan are stocking up on firewood for the Fourth of July. Every house on Duncan comes with a functional fireplace. Guests, turned Icelandic blue in the simple act of grabbing a hamburger off the patio grill, need a roaring fire to defrost and survive summer in this part of the City.

Half the gay men I've ever known in San Francisco live on Duncan. So do Tony and John.

Like the fool I sometimes think I am, I did call Tony at Walton Square. He sounded happy to hear from me and actually enthusiastic about my offer to talk over the lawsuit. Anyone else with an ounce of sense would have heard deafening alarm bells go off in her head when he suggested I come to their house for dinner rather than meet in some publicly neutral place. But I instinctively liked Tony. John was another story, but, for the sake of argument, I decided I didn't know him well enough to make any judgment about him, either pro or con. All told, I opted to ignore conventional wisdom about marching into a lion's den without a stun gun and cheerfully accepted his invitation.

Certainly his gesture was gracious, and I'm a sucker for graciousness, especially when the promise of good food is thrown in. I was sure my instincts were right. He just had to be an innocent in this mess, albeit an innocent I hoped would have information I'd very much like to have.

When I saw the location of their house, however, I wondered if I might possibly be wrong about the assumption of blamelessness. Not only is the street itself cut into the actual rock of Twin Peaks, but their house, in particular, looked glued to the very side of the cliff. The front walk was steep. Probably a pre–Native American, paved-over mountain goat trail, I decided. It did cross my mind at that point that the invitation had really been a clever plot to kill me off, suitably with a heart attack. As I parked in their driveway and looked straight up at their bay window at least twenty feet above the street, for the first time in twenty-five years I wished I were twenty-five years younger.

Fortunately, I'm rarely vain. By the time I reached their front door, my hair was flat with sweat, my clothes looked like I had just stepped out of a swimming pool, and I was panting like a cow that's jogged a mile home to the barn.

John opened the door. He held a cleaver in his hand.

I gasped.

"You're not Jo," he snapped.

I checked quickly. No blood was on the knife, just a sliver of mushroom.

"Alice, actually," I said with an amazingly steady voice.

"Believe me, I'd never confuse the two of you. Come in." He stood back and waved the cleaver toward the inside of the house.

I've had warmer welcomes.

I lurched past him, keeping him firmly in sight from the corner of my eye, and fell heavily but strategically into the nearest chair with a view of the front door as well as the city. It never hurts to mix practicality with pleasure, I always say.

"Want a drink?"

"Water. Please."

"Evian, Ty Nant, San Pellegrino, or domestic."

Having gotten over my initial shock at the sight of the knife, I was relaxing just enough to be irritated by John's pompous tone of voice. I wasn't sure whether this hid a basic social shyness or was more suggestive that he was just your basic ass.

"Evian. Chilled. With a twist." If pomposity was his game, he had just met his match. My mother had managed to train me well in some of the finer social skills.

"Tony! One chilled Frenchie with jaundice for our guest."

Certain conventional wisdom says that gay men are supposed to be witty. Maybe John wasn't really gay.

"What a unique image," I said with my mouth appropriately pursed to signify utter distaste.

"In case you want to know, Ty Nant with lemon is Welsh piss. Pelligrino…"

I held up my hand.

Tony arrived with the Evian just in time.

"I hate to think what you call tap water," I said to Tony, assuming him to be the saner of the two.

"Sewage," Tony said with a smile. "We wouldn't serve that to our worst enemy."

"Glad to hear it."

Tony handed me the cool, damp glass. "You're not the enemy, Alice. I was touched when you called. Lorenza Galli is lucky to have such a caring friend. I like that." Despite the uncanny resemblance to his father, Tony had a nice smile.

"I hate the idea of lawyers fighting out something that straight-forward talking would solve just as well." That part was at least honest of me.

John snorted and headed back to the kitchen.

Tony nodded at his lover and shrugged his shoulders. "I couldn't agree more. But sometimes lawyers make it easier to talk when two parties are too emotionally involved to do it directly, or at least when one of the parties has too much invested to look at the situation objectively and the other is too upset."

I smiled. At this point, I just wanted to be a sweet, agreeable, middle-aged lady—with big ears.

"Tell you what. Let's eat, have a little good wine, relax with some music, and then we can say what we need to say to each other about the legal business."

I nodded enthusiastically. Tony loaded up the CD player with some Brendel Beethoven, Mullova/Canino Bach, and Ashkenazy Chopin before he topped off my Evian and followed John into the kitchen.

I decided that Peters père might have been more likable if he'd smiled like his son.

CHAPTER 17

SERVED IN THE living room with the shifting brown, gold, and red hues of the city below us, dinner was a delight. The first course to arrive was in a huge wooden bowl filled with multitextured fresh leafy things in purple and dark green, garden-fresh tomatoes in red and yellow with sea-green cucumbers as crisp as water chestnuts, all tossed with a light vinaigrette. Behind Tony came John with large, individual wooden bowls and a bottle of sauvignon blanc.

Tony handed me a generous helping. "I hate salads that slop all over the table from flat plates. Fresh leaves don't lie level. They stand up, take up room. You need big bowls." Then he handed me a small but sharp fork that looked like a cross between a salad and a pickle fork. "John designed and made these. They're easier to use so you don't have to chase your lettuce all over the table."

John may not have been witty, but he certainly had a way with sharp things. This miniature pitchfork was a distinct improvement over the traditional salad fork. I complimented him.

"Just the Paul Revere of the '90s!" he crowed.

Well, maybe not quite that good, but I smiled. As long as John kept his mouth shut, with his chiseled features, broad shoulders, and narrow hips, he really did resemble a Greek god. With mouth open, however...well, he should opt to keep the illusion. Meanwhile, I began crunching happily away on my salad while pushing away visions of what else John might be capable of with sharp instruments.

"This is wonderful." I sipped the gently sharp, golden liquid and began to glow inside. "So is the wine."

"It was one of Dad's favorites," Tony said.

I looked at him carefully. He was staring into his wineglass with the intensity of someone who doesn't want to show emotion but feels too much not to direct it somewhere.

"You really loved your father," I said as gently as I could.

Tony blinked quickly but missed the tear rolling down his cheek. John took his hand, tenderly squeezed it, then scowled at me.

"It's okay," Tony said to his partner, and looked up. "Yes, I did. A lot of people hated him. I did too, sometimes. He was a hard man to love."

"A very misunderstood one!" John growled. I could see why they didn't need a dog.

Tony laughed. "You are my dad's biggest fan!" He bent his head affectionately in his lover's direction. "If it hadn't been for John, my father and I probably would never have made peace."

I temporarily filed away that interesting comment, but I didn't want to get sidetracked from Peters while I had Tony talking about him.

"I was a regular reader of your father's column, but I didn't know much about him, other than the divorce from your mother." I hoped that got me good information without sounding like I was fishing for any.

"Wasn't that a gossip columnist's dream!" John rolled his eyes dramatically roofward.

"Dad never was much for pulling punches. And Mother's drinking was pretty impressive. She hid it well, though, even from me. When I defended her after that column of Dad's, it was John who pointed out the number of single-malt Scotch bottles in her trash. I never saw her drunk when I was growing up. When she didn't come home for dinner or wasn't up for breakfast, I assumed it all had something to do with her being a doctor and keeping odd hours. My father never said much to me about her drinking, even later, although he did blame the distance that grew between them solely on the booze, rightly or wrongly. She was brilliant but never got a handle on the liquor problem. She died of cirrhosis of the liver, you know."

I thought back on the article Peters had written, hinting at his wife's drinking. Maybe a newspaper column wasn't the right venue and his approach was, without question, both crass and lacking in compassion, but he hadn't lied. That may not be much to his credit, but it was more than I had given him.

"But I thought the suit was dropped because your father said he wasn't referring to your mother in his column."

"Libel laws are real loose. Normally, it's hard to win, but Mother had a good attorney. She was also the one in the family with the money and social influence. Dad was the son of poor immigrants. Call it rich man's justice, but she could have wiped Dad all over the map and probably stuffed his career down the sewer for him too. But all she wanted was her reputation back."

John snorted and poured himself more wine. "Your Dad got fucked is what happened. He was absolutely right about your mother, but he had to back down or lose his job."

"Not quite, although knowing lawyers, her attorney probably did drop a subtle hint like that to Dad's attorney and then said they'd drop the suit if Dad made it a matter of public record that Mother was a paragon of virtue. Dad's attorney told him he'd agree if he was smart."

"Is the lawsuit what caused the rift between you and your father?" I asked.

"Damned right!" John answered.

Tony reached out and ruffled his lover's hair as if he were a cherished but unruly pet. Did John remind me more of a Rottweiler or a well-trimmed standard poodle?

"That's when I went back to our original surname and stopped talking to Dad. I thought he was out to get Mother. John did set me right on that, but I've long since made peace with both parents. None of us is perfect, after all."

Tony was being more generous to his parents than I would have been.

"But I can't imagine the whole experience didn't have some kind of effect on your father. I kind of got the impression he wasn't too fond of women in the restaurant business for one," I said.

"You're probably right. Dad never forgave my mother. He'd always hated being bested by women. In this case, two women outdid him. Mother's attorney was a woman." Tony laughed.

John got up, rubbed Tony's bald spot with great fondness, and headed for the kitchen. "We better get the second course before you start in on grandma stories."

"Oh, Grandmama! Yes!" Tony's eyes sparkled.

"Tony, I need help…"

"I'll tell you later, Alice." And Tony disappeared into the kitchen.

Course two came bubbling from the oven in a large white casserole. I began drooling (as politely as possible) as soon as I smelled it coming. It was a riot of color that complimented the salad: purple Japanese eggplant, dark green zucchini, red tomatoes, all lightly covered with mozzarella cheese and garlic bread crumbs. The sauvignon blanc disappeared, and John replaced it with a chilled chardonnay from the Napa Valley.

I took one bite. "I've died and gone to food heaven," I said happily. This was family food, warm and loving, joyful and giving. I was beginning to feel guilty. I had hardly come as a real and trusted friend.

"Grandmama's recipe. Dad's mother. That's where he got his interest in food."

"Hang onto your seats," John twittered in a horrible falsetto.

"Sounds interesting," I replied with superb control, as I imagined using John's salad fork on some crucial part of his anatomy. I did want to hear more about Tony's father and ease into Emma before the cock crowed tomorrow morning.

"Dad was an only child, born on the boat before his parents arrived from Italy. His father deserted the family when Dad was about five. Grandmama was not only illiterate but knew maybe two words of English. But she sure knew her way around a stove and got work as a short-order cook flipping burgers to support the two of them. For that, you didn't need much English beyond 'rare, medium-well, and hold the mayo.' At night, she went to school to learn to read and speak English. She never got a high school diploma, but she did start getting better-paying jobs cooking in more upscale restaurants."

"How did she manage all that with a five-year-old?" I took another bite of the family casserole. Pity Grandmama Petroni wasn't the right age for the TV-dinner generation. She'd have made a mint packaging this stuff frozen.

"No choice. Her first priority was to learn to read, write, and speak English like someone born in the States. She actually told Dad she might as well drown the two of them in the bay if she didn't."

"That sounds a bit extreme."

"Not during the Depression. The Anglos took one look at her olive skin, black hair, and brown eyes, and all they saw was someone who'd work for cheap and take a job away from 'an American.' Then the war came, and no one was going to hire an Italian. Obviously, she had good reason to be here rather than back in the old country, but people don't have a lot of sense in wartime. Did you know Italian noncitizens were interned during World War II?"

"No! Japanese, yes. Germans and Italians, no."

"Germans had the right skin color," John muttered as he swallowed some more wine, "and a lot of people liked the Nazi politics."

For a split second, I liked John.

"So, Grandmama couldn't afford to take any chances, and since she didn't have any family here, she did it all herself. She took Dad with her. If he cried, whined, or caused any problems, she whipped the shorts off him and told him he'd make them both starve. Dad told me her favorite threat was: 'You cry, you die.' But she got citizenship papers just under the wire. And they didn't starve."

I'd have called that awfully close to child abuse, but what did I know? I'd never had to worry about starving. Nor had I ever faced being put into an internment camp for some irrational reason that no child—or intelligent adult—would ever understand. At least I hadn't had to worry yet. I thought about the movement not that long ago to confine AIDS victims in quarantine camps and how many people still thought homosexuality was taught, not innate.

"And despite all that, Tony's father never once raised a hand to his son. I find that pretty impressive." John raised a glass to the absent Peters.

"True," Tony said. "But it didn't make him the easiest person to be around or the nicest, especially to women."

"But why take it out on other women? His mother was only trying to survive. How did he do that?" Not that I couldn't figure it out, but we might be getting somewhere interesting, and I wanted to encourage Tony.

"Spoken like a true defender of the gentler sex." John was now raising his glass to me, but his unblinking dark eyes held no look of affection.

"You need a cigarette, Honeybuns." Tony stood up and stretched. "Why don't you go out on the deck, do your drug, and come back civilized. Alice and I'll keep the good stories until you get back."

John grabbed a fresh pack of Marlboros and marched out. At least he glared at each of us equally.

"Ignore him, Alice. We've been together nearly fifteen years, and he really is much sweeter than he's being tonight."

Sweet? John? Could've fooled me. Considering what I'd seen of him in general and his temper in specific, I was beginning to think John was a close second cousin to Ivan the Terrible. Did Tony really think I was going to take his testimonial as objective and on faith?

"Maybe he doesn't like redheaded women," I said. Or maybe he doesn't care much for women in general, I thought, just like his apparent hero, Peters.

"He had just finished his weekly chat with his mother not long before you got here."

And that was supposed to explain why he greeted me at the door with a cleaver in hand?

"She still calls him her baby son and wants to know when he's going to grow up and find a nice girl to marry."

"And I remind him of his mother." How utterly and boringly Freudian, I thought. "Would she be an overweight redhead by any chance?"

Tony blushed. "She does have red hair—dyed."

"Natural." I ran my hand through my hair, which had dried into an unruly mass of short curls, and showed him that no color had rubbed off.

"But she doesn't look a bit like you."

I'll bet.

"She's a bitter woman whose fourth husband just left her because he was tired of competing for space in bed with the junk food."

"Fat."

"Obese. Alice, it's just the hair color that reminds John of his mother!"

Tony was beginning to fidget uneasily. Since I both liked and needed him, I ceased the needling. "It's okay," I laughed. "I don't eat junk food, and I'm not on my fourth husband."

He smiled and picked up a wineglass. We toasted each other and sat quietly, waiting for Honeybuns to return.

It was that special time of evening in the city when night lights come on and twinkle in the heated air, but the day and its colors hang on and on as if life itself depended on it. Most people seem to love this time. I hate it. It depresses me. I don't want days to fade and hang on like a sick old age with no joy. I want them to end as vibrantly and alive as they began. That way I can always believe another day will be there when I wake up the next morning. But, as Frances once said to me, no being had asked my opinion on the matter when the world was created, and no being was likely to now. I bit my lip.

Tony sighed, breaking my mood. "You know," he said, "I really think Dad loved Mother. I hope I'm not saying this because I want it to be true. But after Grandmama, he was afraid of competent women. He never wanted to be controlled by one again, but he was drawn to them too. And Mother certainly was competent. The drinking came later in life, I found out. After I was born. And sometimes I think he used it as his excuse to escape from her. To my knowledge, he never tried to help her or suggest she get help. He just left. After her, he told me he'd never marry again. And the only women he got involved with after the divorce were ones he could control, like his girlfriend Jo."

"What was the reason he didn't like women chefs or restaurant owners? Competence? His mother cooked but…"

"Oh, I think it was mostly Grandmama. She eventually remarried a guy who owned a restaurant in North Beach. When he died, he left her the place, which included a flat over the shop, so to speak. She did a bang-up business for years until she literally couldn't walk upstairs anymore. Dad refused to take it on. Maybe he was afraid he couldn't match her success. She sold it, moved to a nursing home, and died a month later."

John marched into the room and plopped himself into a chair next to Tony. "But he was always fair. He never panned a woman who didn't deserve it," he said.

Like Lorenza? To calm my rising temper, I repeated the mantra "John is sweet. John is sweet. Like coated with molasses and tied to an anthill…"

"There was the business with Emma," Tony said, passing the wine bottle around.

Now we were getting somewhere!

So now, of course, was when the doorbell rang.

CHAPTER 18

THE WOMAN IN the doorway was dressed in shimmering black. The neckline on her close-fitting sheath plunged so far it almost met her hem, which circled somewhere about the middle of her thighs.

I quickly reached for my wineglass.

"Hi, Jo! Come on in." John was smiling ear to ear.

"Hello, handsome," the woman cooed as she softly brushed her lips against his.

Tony stood up and pointed in my direction. "This is Alice Mc-Doughall. Jo Morgan."

Oh, I remembered her all right. How could I forget the Marilyn Monroe look-alike? Gone were the fragility and haunted vulnerability I thought I had seen just before Peters died. Tonight she oozed sex appeal by the simple act of breathing. The effect on me was amazingly immediate. Had I been years younger, I would have assumed my body had just been covered in napalm. But having passed the half-century, I was only afraid my heart wouldn't take all this pounding.

I needn't have worried. Her cold and instantly dismissive glance at my overripe breasts, generous waist, and ample belly were like snow on my fire. To save pride, I reminded myself that I had once been of similar litheness and knew from experience what would happen to all those soft little curves of hers. I admit, however, that I did suck in my stomach just a bit.

"Hi," I said.

She nodded briefly and turned back to John, whom she casually caressed from shoulder to wrist. I must admit I was a little surprised. Surely she knew he and Tony were a couple. Perhaps the gesture was more automatic than deliberately seductive? Perchance she was just keeping in practice. Or maybe this was just the way she was with all the men she knew…

"Am I late for din-din," she breathed.

"As always." John laughed and gently removed her hand.

She pouted. "Ooh."

"But there's plenty left—and still hot," Tony said.

"Just a wittle salad, ToneTone. Please?" She indicated a hair's breadth with her fingers. "I really couldn't eat much." She glanced quickly in my direction with what I interpreted as mild disgust. "And a little glass of wine. You know, I'm just so depressed."

Why both Tony and John had to leave to get her "wittle" salad and small glass of wine, I don't know. I was not pleased to be left alone with this woman.

I smiled with grim grace.

She ignored my attempt at sociability, perched herself on the arm of Tony's chair, crossed her legs, and began to swing one nervously. I half expected her to pull out a nail file, hairbrush, or lipstick to while away her time.

"I am deeply sorry about your loss," I said, trying to be nice and managing to sound stilted.

She glanced up at me with surprise, as if she had forgotten I was even there. "You wouldn't know anything about it," she said.

I felt anger burning all the way up my neck into my face until my eyes began to hurt with it. Instead of having a stroke, I bit my tongue.

John and Tony came back with a fresh bottle of chardonnay, a large bowl of salad, and a pasta dish full of dinner.

"Hope you can enjoy just a bit of this, Jo." Tony poured her a large glass of wine, and John put the food down on the table in front of her.

Jo tucked into her food like a starving truck driver. I watched with wicked satisfaction. Indeed, her appetite boded well for the future expansion of all those little curves she was so proud of.

Tony gestured toward me with the wine bottle. I took a hefty glassful.

"Did I interrupt anything, boys?" Even rude and with her mouth full, Jo managed to exude an irresistible musk.

"We were just talking about Dad's reviews. Do you remember the one he did on Emma?"

"Remind me, ToneTone. Who was she?"

"She was the owner of The Bountiful Harvest."

"The Bountiful Harvest?" I sputtered, nearly choking on my wine. "I remember that place! It was a knockout. We all loved it. In fact, I think Lorenza patterned…" I stopped myself quickly. There were a few things I didn't need to say in this particular company. Lorenza had always admired that restaurant and did use several ideas from it for The Lovage. But Emma as owner of The Bountiful Harvest? Could it really be our Emma? I was stunned.

"There were so many your dad and I went to, honey. This one just isn't standing out."

"Vegetarian and seafood. One of the first nonethnic restaurants in the city without beef or fowl on the menu," John said.

"Oh, now I remember! It was really awful." Jo rolled her eyes, swallowed half her wine, and passed the glass to Tony for a refill.

"But it was fabulous," I said, almost to myself.

"It was," Tony said. "Emma really worked hard on that place. But when Dad went to review it the first time, she bombed. The second time he went, it was even worse."

Jo began to giggle. "It was really, really bad! It was almost funny, the food was so terrible."

"Your father was right in everything he said about that place, Tony. You just couldn't see it because you grew up with Emma Stilwell, and you were close friends. You had no perspective." John was beginning to pick up our plates.

Jo signaled for a second helping on the casserole.

"I ate there other times. It was good." Tony looked sad.

"It was." I may have nodded empathetically to support Tony, but I was numb with shock over the news of the restaurant owner.

"Boy, did what's-her-name fool you, ToneTone!" Jo waved her hand playfully. "The first time we went, your dad ordered pasta primavera. It was supposed to be the specialty of the house. When it came, I almost threw up. It looked like congealed worms with watery tomato sauce and a couple of chopped carrots for garnish."

Well, give the woman credit; she could make you see it. I swallowed hard.

John came back with another bowl of the casserole and handed it to Jo. "And the second time the food was even shoddier," he said. "It took ages to get the attention of someone on the wait staff. Then the food was stone cold when we got it."

"Ooo! It was horrible!" Jo bounced up and down in the chair with an almost childish glee. I couldn't help but notice that her hemline had slipped upward to a length unacceptable even on San Francisco streets. At least she was wearing underwear. I blushed anyway.

Tony was shaking his head. "I never understood what happened."

"Why didn't you ask her? John said you were good friends." I reached for the chardonnay. The fresh bottle was empty. Jo had done quite well for herself with the wine. So much for just one small glass.

"I tried." He hesitated. "But she disappeared."

CHAPTER 19

"HOW?" I ASKED.

"Poof!" Jo was waving her hands in circles over her head. She was drunk.

"I don't know," Tony said. "I called and called but only got the answering machine. Then the machine stopped taking messages. I went to her apartment, but a strange guy answered the door and told me she must have moved because he had been living there a month."

"Does she have family here?" I asked.

"Under a rock. Falling like a rock? Love me like a rock!" Jo began to sing as she swung one crossed leg in an off-sync rhythm.

"A mother, but they had a rocky relationship. After Emma's father committed suicide, they were left with tons of bills, so her mother took in boarders to save the house and went to work as a sales clerk at The Emporium. Emma had always wanted to be a chef, but her mother told her that she should just get a job after high school until she got married. She managed to persuade her mother that learning to cook would be a good skill in the marriage market, so she was able to finish the culinary course at City College. Once she started work, she gave her mother money but moved out as soon as she could. They, ah, had a falling out around then, so I think the monthly check was about their only contact. When I called, her mother didn't know where she was. She actually sounded worried. I guess Emma had stopped sending money."

"And you haven't heard from her since?" I asked.

Tony shook his head.

"Would it surprise you to know that she is the executive chef at The Lovage in Livorno?"

"What!"

Well, if I were any judge of people at all, I'd be in no doubt that Tony was utterly shocked with my news. John, on the other hand, was looking a tad pale. Jo was ignoring the whole conversation and softly doing a medley of greatest hits from the '80s, not that I really cared what she did as long as she didn't interrupt right now.

"John, did you know this?" Tony's face was turning a mottled red.

"Yes."

"And you didn't tell me. Why?"

"After the way she treated you, her childhood buddy? The guy she almost married for Christ's sake! She walks away without a word and has no contact for how many years? Come on, Tony, you didn't need her back in your life."

"Married?" Now that was an interesting development.

"Married. The rift between Emma and her mother happened when she told her we had 'broken up.' Emma and I realized in time that we loved each other but that both of us were queer. When she told her mother she was a lesbian, her mother had a fit. Short version of a long story," was Tony's quick aside to me.

Emma? Nature's gift to men, a lesbian? Do run that one past me again!

"Shouldn't it be my decision whether or not I want to get in touch?" Tony was trying very hard to keep his voice level in the presence of company, but he was clearly furious with John.

"I'm sorry I upset you. I thought I was doing the right thing." John actually looked like he was going to cry.

"Sometimes you try to protect me too much. You're not my father."

Jo began to hum a song I didn't know her generation even knew. Then she put some words to it: "I want a boy just like the boy who married dear, dear daddy! La. La."

Not quite the right words, but maybe she wasn't that far off. John did remind me all too much of Peters. But, in the meantime, Tony and John were in each other's arms. John was sobbing and getting his lover's shirt wet.

"Go smoke, Honeybuns. It's okay. I love you. You meant well."

John got up, grabbed some tissues out of Tony's shirt pocket, and went out sniffling.

"I guess I shouldn't have said anything."

"Alice, there is a lot of history here you had no way of knowing. I wanted to know where Emma was, so you did the right thing. John will get over it."

"This woman. The one who gave us worms for dinner. She was at the place way out in the country too? It was such a long drive! I don't know why we had to go all the way out there. I tried to talk Artie out of it," Jo giggled.

I wish you had, I thought grimly.

CHAPTER 20

AFTER JOHN CAME back, we settled into distracting conversation, carefully avoiding any further mention of Emma or Peters Senior. Jo began to successfully monopolize the rest of the evening like a spoiled child movie star. And like adults waiting for the parents to show up and take responsibility, we all avoided any confrontation and humored her.

She flirted with John. Flattered Tony outrageously. Followed both to the kitchen, where I could hear her *ooh*'ing and *ah*'ing over everything in the refrigerator until they gave her samples to take home. Me, of course, she ignored as much as possible. And finally, about eleven o'clock, she left—after having borrowed "just a few dollars to tide her over" until she could start the job at Nordstrom downtown. That "few dollars" translated into three digits from what I thought I saw Tony give her. The whole performance made me wonder who had really controlled whom in the Peters/Jo relationship.

Even though none of us said anything after she left, I suspected we all pretty much felt the same. Jo had worn us out.

"DINNER WAS WONDERFUL, Tony. And I really loved the sorbets, John." I even meant my compliment. He had given each of us a plate filled with small balls of homemade and perfectly flavored sorbets for dessert. Jo had served them and, for some reason, I got a lot of the coconut. It tasted perfectly of coconut. Of course, I hate coconut.

"We didn't get to talk much about the lawsuit," Tony said. "Sorry. Jo often shows up for meals now that Dad's gone. I guess she's feeling pretty lost. After all the years they were together, she's had to find a job. He spent everything he had and left her only a few thousand and a car. He didn't even have a condo. They each had their own apartments. It's not easy. John and I try to help."

And he left his son nothing either? I couldn't help but wonder.

"She won't stay single for long. Your dad thought she was pretty hot stuff in the sack." John waved in the direction of the kitchen. "Anyone for coffee?"

I yawned discretely and nodded vigorously. "Maybe we don't need to discuss it much. Lorenza did not do the burrito entrée your father ate that night. Emma was in charge of the kitchen. But Lorenza hasn't been able to ask her what happened. Emma's been in and out of the hospital. Whatever burrito filling your father ate was definitely not one of Lorenza's recipes, and she has no idea where the idea came from. It had to have been Emma's. At least that's what I think."

"Hospital?"

Why did everyone hone in on that and totally ignore what Emma may have been doing the night of Peters's death? Nothing stuck to her. I was beginning to think she would have a great future in politics. "She had a bit of an accident. Ran into a burglar. But she'll be okay and back to work full-time soon."

John returned with a large coffee press, something that looked like real cream and sugar, plus three mugs on a tray. "Cream? Sugar?" he asked. "Hey, I'm sorry to hear about Emma's problems, but I sure would like to know what she thought she was doing that night. The whole salad/burrito thing reminds me of a repeat of her canned spaghetti. I guess I'm really not surprised to hear she was the one in charge that night, not your friend."

Well, thank you, John!

"But Emma was better than that!"

And then we have Tony, her loyal friend.

"Let's not fight over this again. Maybe she was, but she sure screwed up the two times your father was at The Bountiful Harvest, and she apparently did again at The Lovage. I am really not imagining this. I was there all three times."

This was like being at a tennis match. I turned to Tony for his reply.

"You were the one who wanted to sue Alice's friend."

Back to John.

"I thought she had planned the menu and done the recipes."

In this company, I thought honesty might win more points. "Lorenza did do the menu and the recipes, but someone changed the burrito filling from what had been planned. Neither Lorenza nor her sous-chef did that. It may have been Emma. Lorenza just hasn't been able to find out." I hoped no one would ask for a timeline showing Emma's periodic, albeit rare and very brief, appearances at The Lovage, when Lorenza actually could have questioned her more carefully had she not cared more for Emma's health than the dubious stuffing. In the cold world of law, Lorenza's warmhearted gesture would still appear negligent.

Tony and John were looking at each other in that special, silent discussion that only longtime, close couples can effectively conduct.

"Maybe *you* could talk to Emma about what happened, Tony." I didn't think another little nudge in a direction away from Lorenza would hurt.

"I don't want to do that. She's the one who stayed out of touch."

"But why go after Lorenza? She was innocent." Not strictly true. It was still her restaurant. She was the one in charge. But since it was John's idea to sue out of some need to avenge the death of a man he clearly admired, maybe his anger could be redirected to Emma. He already thought she had treated his Tony badly, and he had seen her failures before.

"I never wanted to do this anyway," Tony said.

John looked at me with a slight frown. "Money was never the issue here. Suing was the only way I felt there could be some justice for Tony's father. He had his faults, but he treated us like the couple we are and got me started in my accounting business with his restaurant buddies. I owe him, goddammit, and he sure didn't deserve what happened."

"So you'll drop the suit?" I looked at John hopefully.

"No."

"Why?" I asked, as calmly as I could. I was so sure I had been close to a resolution. Suddenly I felt bone tired.

"Maybe."

Make up your mind, Honeybuns, I thought, before I claw your eyes out in sheer frustration.

"Can you get Emma to call us?" John asked.

"Of course." Now that I could promise. At this point, I was ready to tie her to the phone without food or water until she called Tony and John just to save Lorenza any more angst.

"If she can explain what happened that night and it's clear your friend wasn't involved, then maybe it would be fair enough to drop any suit against The Lovage."

I almost could have hugged John.

"I think Emma would be more than happy to tell you what happened." And, if not now, she will be by the time I finish laying a major guilt trip on her about what she's doing to that wonderful person who, she has admitted, gave her a chance to get back into the restaurant world.

"Deal?" John looked at Tony.

"Deal," Tony and I said in unison.

IT WAS PAST midnight in the city when I got up to leave, but before I did, I asked Tony if he had copies of the reviews his father had written on the Bountiful Harvest. He looked at me a bit doubtfully at first but then seemed willing enough to pull them out of his files and photocopy them for me. Hopefully, I could find something in those reviews to help me twist Emma's arm into taking full blame in this fiasco.

With the reviews folded and tucked into my purse, I hugged Tony good-bye and shook John's hand. Since he had turned out to be of more help than hindrance, I decided not to force on John a hug from an obese, redheaded woman, even if she wasn't his mother.

CHAPTER 21

NEVER FEED CATS in the morning if you want to sleep late on a weekend. I remember being given that advice years ago when Frances and I adopted our first alarm clocks with hair. Unfortunately, that same wise individual, whose name I've fortuitously forgotten, failed to say that cats, with perfectly good feline logic, would wake you when they wanted to. After all, if you're crazy enough to get up early for five days, why not for seven?

That I had arrived home after one in the morning and fallen into bed after two meant zilch to my little angels. Well, perhaps not totally zero. Normally, they will allow some sleeping in. However, by nine, they had had enough of liberal solicitude and positioned themselves next to my head, both jammed into the space between my chin and eyebrows. I therefore awoke to their somewhat discordant purrs and the stale smell of whatever I gave them for dinner last night. I was less than grateful.

Usually, I prefer a good eight to nine hours of sleep each night. Less, and I'm raggedy. Add a bit more wine the night before than I should have drunk, and I think you could honestly say I wasn't exactly America's vision of the perfectly happy citizen that morning. My day had definitely not started well.

But I did hug my feline friends, slide out of bed with a clunk, and gingerly head toward the bathtub for a long soak, deliberately ignoring the blinking light on my answering machine. The warm bath definitely improved the situation, as did a large glass of orange juice. Finally, I sat down, picked up a pencil, and pushed the message button.

BEEP: "Alice? Angel. Please call me at your convenience. Home number: 897-4506." Click. (At my convenience? At my pleasure! I wonder if my handsome, inexplicably heterosexual detective is awake yet?)

BEEP: "Mr. Stewart, please call Dr. Watson's office. It's very important." Click. (Stewart may be Scottish, but it's a long way from McDoughall. I hope Watson listens to his patients better than his staff does to answering-machine introductions.)

BEEP: "Dano! Come on down! You're missing some world-class knockers, buddy!" Clunka-click. (Poor Dano. Probably missed the opportunity of a lifetime.)

BEEP: "Alice. Call me." Click. (Dear Lorenza. Succinct as ever.)

The tape had just rewound and my pencil was still hovering over the last message when the phone rang.

"Yes," I snapped. My usually sweet disposition hadn't quite returned.

"Why didn't you call me when you got in?" On the other hand, Lorenza sounded more worried than annoyed.

"Lorenza, it was one in the morning."

"Yeah? Well, it's now after ten. Are you up?"

"No, I'm fast asleep. What do you think?"

"Alone?"

"Edward and Piers are here. You know I have no secrets from them."

"I thought you were out on a date last night."

"Look, I'm not a kid anymore. I may fall more heavily into bed than I used to, but I don't fall as quickly."

At least that got a chuckle. "So it didn't work out."

"I wasn't on a date! I spent the evening with Tony Petroni and significant appendage, trying to get you off the hook on the lawsuit. And I may have come up with a way to do it. For this, I overate, overdrank, and slaved over the negotiation table to the wee hours of the morning, only to be awakened at the veritable crack of dawn by sarcasm."

"The crack was five hours ago."

"Interpreted, that means you're grateful."

"Yes. And you are the best friend anyone could ever have."

"I don't feel the earth move from your jumps of joy."

"Alice, I'm in a real rush. I am grateful, but I need you to do a…well, another favor for me. Something came up at the restaurant, and I'm tied up. I promised to take some food up to Emma for her to try out on lunch and dinner today but just can't make it. Would you mind?"

"Would I mind…"

"You're a real sweetheart! Drop by as soon as you can. Elena will have it all packaged and ready to go. I really am thrilled with the news, but the repair guy just showed up. Can't talk now."

"Sure—"

"You're a life saver!" And she hung up.

I stared at the humming receiver. Well, Lorenza, old friend, you may not have realized it, but you just gave me the perfect excuse to go harass a recuperating cook.

CHAPTER 22

AS I HUNG up the phone, a gloomy mood unexpectedly fell over me like a drab blanket. I could have blamed it on the hangover, I guess. Since Frances's death, I occasionally drink more than I should, last night not being as rare an occasion as I would like to admit. Drinking as a response to her death might seem an odd reaction, perhaps, considering that a drunk driver killed her. However, despite my brusque façade of certainty about life and people, I do understand that humans aren't always as rational as cats. And, in the solitude of those silent nights when sleep escapes me, I step back and remember that good and evil in anyone, myself included, are often relative.

On the other hand, maybe the mood was caused by my rather divergent feelings over what I had discovered last night about Emma. Contrary to what I would have liked to think, she had actually been the owner and chef of one of the best new restaurants in San Francisco several years ago. The buzz at the time suggested she was headed for legendary status in the business.

Then she bombed. Certainly Peters thought she did, and both John and Jo corroborated his opinion. Yet Tony, Frances, Lorenza, George, and I had all thought it was a knockout success. Lorenza has told me it was her inspiration in many ways.

That also meant Lorenza must have known who Emma was when she hired her as chef. It would certainly explain her defense of Emma's culinary skills and perhaps even her loyalty in the face of a bizarre entrée disaster. I did find it odd Lorenza had never told me about the connection. But that was a personal issue between Lorenza and me, which I planned to deal with soon.

Meanwhile, with this new information, more questions began to buzz through my head like mosquitoes. That disaster at The Lovage was very reminiscent of what had happened to our Emma at her own place, a curious repeat for someone so badly burned the first time around. And why was Emma late getting to The Lovage the night of Peters's review when prior experience would have told her to get there earlier, not later? And why did she throw out the burrito filling as soon as she knew Peters had dropped dead? What did she know and whom was she really trying to protect? Was it actually Lorenza and Elena? She readily admitted she had done it. That hardly suggests she was protecting herself.

As I got dressed, I also thought about Tony's tales of his father. I tried to decide whether Peters could have been simply vindictive with his bad reviews of The Bountiful Harvest or if he had been as maliciously honest as he had been about his wife's drinking.

No way am I qualified to unravel anyone's mental Gordian knot, but surely Peters paid some price for the beatings his mother gave him. Without question, she handled a difficult situation with courage and grit. But how sad that society couldn't have taken the wartime blinders off, given her a hand, and thus spared the child bruises he never recovered from.

I don't doubt for a minute that Peters was terrified of competent women and wanted to protect himself from more of same. But he married one. What acid reaction that mating produced, driving the one to drink and chasing the other away. There is a story I'll never know. I wonder if even their son does. But the fact remained, he did actually fall in love and marry a woman who was more than the "yes dear" type. And after the divorce, he seemed to have knowingly attached himself to women he could control.

Jo must have been perfect. She was the ideal accessory for a man no longer young who wanted the world to know he could still satisfactorily bed a "looker" and do so for a period of time. Of course, I wonder whether he would have pensioned her off or traded her in when she got her first wrinkle. If she normally ate and drank at the rate I saw last night, that first wrinkle might not have been far off. But I'll be generous: Maybe he wouldn't have. And maybe I was just a little envious of Jo, irrational as that may be.

Bottom line here: He was aware enough to know that he couldn't handle the competent women, so he chose the weaker vessels of the female sex, like Jo. If he was that aware, maybe he knew what he was doing with his reviews. Maybe he was still crude, vicious, insensitive, and boorish, but also truthful. No law has ever equated truth with kindness. More's the pity, perhaps.

With one shoe on and one still slippered, I limped to my purse. If Peters had indeed told the unvarnished truth about what happened the two nights he reviewed The Bountiful Harvest, there might be a clue to what was behind the disaster at The Lovage and Emma's responsibility for it.

I had my questions; I wanted my answers. So, depressed or not, hangover or no, I put on water for coffee, pulled out the reviews Tony had given me, and began to read. Emma's lunch could wait. She was thin enough. Surely she wouldn't starve for another half hour.

THE REVIEWS WERE vicious. No doubt about that. Like a hunting animal, Peters circled his victim slowly, then lunged for the kill with speed and cunning. Compliments on the elegant simplicity of the interior became the basis for expectation that the same would be true of the meal. He so carefully built up to this presumption that the reader felt what I can only describe as culinary betrayal when he exclaimed, with all the grief of a lover deceived:

I could not believe what had been placed before me. Not fresh pasta caressed by delicate herbs and organic tomatoes redolent of hot sun after the morning dew? Not at all! In the middle of my plate lay a lump of overcooked spaghetti, dotted with ill-defined orange-colored bits and slathered with a tinny flavored sauce whose only claim to freshness was a recent arrival from some can. "Surely," I said to my server, "there must be some mistake? This cannot be pasta primavera!" Alas, the poor man confirmed the worst. It was indeed and had even been "created" by the owner herself. I grieved not only for my party and myself; I grieved also for the owner/chef, Emma Stilwell. Had no one the kindness to disabuse her of any misguided faith in her culinary ability? But perhaps she will yet prove herself and show that tonight was only a glitch in an otherwise fabulous future as a restaurateur. I look forward to coming again and being proven terribly wrong.

Of course, he came again a month later and, of course, found he had not been wrong. If anything, the situation was even worse, and his printed cry of pain hit the reader again and again:

Service? There was none! My poor guests, trusting me to bring them to an exciting adventure in food and atmosphere, waited half an hour before our orders were even taken. The food might have been good had it been hot. Sadly, it was stone cold when it finally reached our table. I wish I could have blamed this on a busy night. Alas, it was slow for a Saturday, much slower than it had been when we last came. Distressed, I asked to speak to the young Chef Emma, who also owns The Bountiful Harvest, thinking she would make all well. But on one of the busiest nights in the business, she was nowhere to be found. Perhaps she's lost interest in her restaurant? My party and I certainly have.

It didn't take the proverbial rocket scientist to see a similarity between serving canned spaghetti to a restaurant critic and putting mashed favas into his burrito. It also didn't take a major stretch of the imagination to see cold food and over-oiled salad coming from the same creative mind.

Fortunately, that creative mind had failed to do in a second restaurant. With luck, I could get this lawsuit dropped and Lorenza would only be out whatever god-awful attorney fees she had to date. If I were really lucky, maybe I could even get Emma to pay those.

Edward chose that moment to wander into the kitchen, sniff, and reject all food left for him on the floor. With a disdainful snort, he glanced up at me and marched back out, tail shaking in ill-disguised contempt. Thus was I kindly reminded that the most logical assumptions to one (I thought there was adequate food for the cat) may be totally erroneous to another (the cat).

Okay, so maybe I was being too simplistic about Emma. What motivations could she have had to seriously mess up two restaurants, one not even her own? And how could I account for her seeming innocence about the lawsuit? And then there was the almost naive protectiveness she had shown Lorenza and Elena by discarding the mixture after Peters died. And what about her own obvious success before…

There were just too many damned questions! I wanted to scream. I was getting obsessed with this. Damn! Damn! Damn!

I slammed my hand down on the table. It hurt like hell. I touched it gingerly. With my luck, I probably broke something.

Edward and Piers stuck their heads around the door to check if I still had sufficient sanity to share the house with them. I wasn't sure I had but waved to them confidently anyway. I felt reassured when they decided it was safe enough to ignore me and disappeared toward my bedroom. I wished my problem with Emma could be so easily dismissed.

WHEN I FINALLY arrived at The Lovage, Lorenza and the repair-person both had their heads in the oven. Elena assured me that, appearance to the contrary, all was going quite well.

So the restaurant might open on time for dinner, but there was no way Lorenza had the time to tell me if she had asked the staff what they knew about the damned filling. Nor could I ask why she had never told me that Emma was a once famous chef.

And, as Elena handed over the container of soup and assorted packages of dishes with warm, spicy fragrances, she smiled and asked me to give Emma her love. Emma had indeed charmed the one other person I had hoped would share my suspicions of the former Bountiful Harvest owner.

CHAPTER 23

THE DRIVE TO Emma's was not for the timid.

Lorenza and I both live in the newer part of town, which is on the top of one of Livorno's hills, but no matter how twisted, our road was still built for the era of the car. Emma had rented a flat in a Victorian in the old part of town. In the 1890s, women in bustles and corsets climbed mountains; men did the same in boiled collars. Considering such absurdity, it was not out of the question, therefore, that the original owners of this house might have had feet permanently slanted at forty-five-degree angles. Certainly they would have needed same to walk up to their house. Any self-respecting horse would have, quite sensibly, balked.

Anyway, by about the 1920s, I would guess, cars came to Livorno, and someone roughed out a road to accommodate his fine new roadster. Being a thrifty lot in this town, the next generation simply paved over the original dirt path and dubbed it "street." Pity they didn't leave behind the wheels of their cars as evidence, because they must have been specially equipped with suction cups, necessary in preventing the car from tipping, hood over tailpipe, into the ocean below.

So far, my ten-year-old Japanese import had successfully clawed its way up to Emma's lodgings but only, I think, because I suggestively whispered "Fujiyama" each time in hopes of invoking happy ancestral memories. I don't like pressing my luck, however.

On the other hand, the view is spectacular. There are days when the air is clear that the colors of the trees, earth, and sea are so vivid they hurt the eyes. Alternately, when storms roll in, everything is washed in countless shades of gray. Then there are times when the houses on the bluff are lost in a kind of *Brigadoon* world as the fog moves in and muffles all sound but the wail of the foghorn located at the entrance to the small bay.

But today my mind was on survival, not on the view behind me, as I willed my overworked car up the road with one hand clutching the steering wheel and the other balancing the soup pot, which was strapped in with a seat belt. Obviously, when something as basic as continued existence is uppermost, only very important things will divert my attention.

Like a sporty little Fiat, with personalized plates stating an enigmatic NORDAMI, parked with open door almost in the middle of the road and from which stuck two bare legs. Two bare female legs. Nice-looking bare female legs. Of course, I noticed that the Fiat was from a San Francisco dealership and because I believe firmly in helping lost tourists, I stomped on the brake, jammed on the emergency, and rolled down the window.

"Need any help?" I asked hopefully.

Now, it is my opinion that the short skirts of the '90s are a vast improvement over the minis of the '60s, when Frances and I got together. Of course, I could never wear minis, being cursed with the Celtic rear, which, translated, means I used to sit on 60 of my then 125 pounds. More women definitely seem to be able to wear the current style, or maybe I'm just noticing more of them.

In any event, the rest of the body had now emerged and certainly fulfilled the promise suggested by the legs. Without question, the short skirt looked good on her, even as she teetered precariously on three-inch heels. I guessed she might be about Lorenza's height in her stocking feet. Thin, but not boyish, she had shoulder-length hair, which was nicely streaked with blond highlights. Her suit was a classic cut, long jacket in off-white linen with a skirt of matching fabric, all tailored to fit easily over every curve without bunching. Strapped over her shoulder was a soft bag, which looked like genuine Italian leather, not home-grown simulated. The only discordant note in this whole picture were the opaque sunglasses in royal blue. I assumed she was looking in my direction but wasn't sure. It's eerie not being able to see someone's eyes.

She had not responded.

"Help? Need any?" I repeated, assuming she hadn't heard me the first time.

She continued to blue-eye me.

I was beginning to feel uncomfortable.

"No," she said finally. "I don't." Her voice was high-pitched and grated on my ear. I was disappointed. The voice shattered an otherwise compelling vision.

"I made a wrong turn." She took off her glasses and waved them at me. "Would you move your car so I can do a U?" Her tone of voice suggested that it was I who had gotten in her way, not vice versa.

Annoyed, I rolled up the window, released my brake, gunned the motor, and shot a few yards past her to the end of the road. As I did so, I realized there was something familiar about the woman. What it was did not come to me until after I had turned myself around and parked. By that time, she had just made a right turn at the bottom of the hill and was happily on her way.

A strange coincidence perhaps, but I couldn't help wondering what John's guest from the night of Peters's death was doing on the street just opposite Emma's flat.

CHAPTER 24

EMMA NOT ONLY rented a flat on the top of the highest hill in Livorno, but she also rented the top flat, and there was no elevator. In addition to dragging my own 222 pounds up the stairs, I had to heft at least 10 pounds of soup and packaged food plus another 5 of purse, shoes, and clothes. Believe me, I was counting every ounce and stair as a special favor to Lorenza by the time I banged at the cook's door with the only thing free: my foot.

"Lorenza's soon-to-be-famous Indian lentil soup," I announced, each word separated by subtle gasps for air, when Emma opened the door.

She reached for the container of soup and packages of food.

"No," I coughed, clutching the container to my sweating bosom. "It's too heavy for you to lift. Where's the kitchen?"

She smiled and pointed. "At the back. Through the living room."

Frugal modernity definitely defined Emma's style of furnishing. I walked around two walnut-colored chairs of Scandinavian simplicity that were in the middle of the room. In between them was a table lamp. That was her sole attempt at living room furniture, but, despite the austere design, the chairs looked comfortable and commanded a great view of the sparkling bay and ocean. To the right, floor-to-ceiling pole bookcases, stuffed full of books, filled one wall. Beyond that, there were no rugs, no pictures, no knick-knacks, no past, no present, no nothing. And something else was missing, something very important.

I slid the soup onto the countertop, hoisted the food up beside it, and sighed.

Of course! There was no pitter-patter of little feline feet. How awful!

"Iced tea?" Emma asked.

I swallowed, nodded, and willed myself back into the living room with what little strength I had left, plunking myself carefully into one of the chairs. Not only was it sturdier than it looked, the thing was definitely comfortable.

"This should help." Emma handed me a tall glass of iced tea. "Let me know if it isn't sweet enough." She stood by my chair while I tried to gulp as quietly as possible.

"Delicious!" Despite my best efforts to be as ladylike as my mother had tried to teach me, I had swigged the entire glass in record time.

"Let me get you some more."

"Don't exert yourself. You're supposed to be resting." I might have some hard questions for her, but I really didn't want her to use up energy waiting on me.

"I can carry one small glass without overdoing." She looked at me with what I might describe as gentle amusement, took my glass, and went back to the kitchen. I felt a twinge of guilt but wasn't exactly sure why.

Although she didn't have much furniture in the living room, the few pieces were new and well made, as if she was buying them piece by piece and to last. Only the books, mostly paperback, looked worn. There hadn't been much in the kitchen either, as I thought about it: herbs growing in a sunny window but no table in the nook, a large brick and board bookcase full of cookbooks but only one cheap pot in the sink.

I tried to remember the bedroom from the first day I had brought her home from the hospital: a single bed, a phone on the floor with a clock radio next to it, some good stereo equipment with a partially filled, small CD tower adjacent to it, and no TV. No TV? How un-American!

Emma returned, handed me a fresh glass of iced tea, and sat in the other chair. Despite the ascetic plainness of what I hesitate to call décor, there was a feeling of warmth and camaraderie about the arrangement of the chairs. I could almost picture two older women sitting in them, one knitting and one reading with that quiet ease people have who have lived together for more years than not. Frances should be in that other chair, I thought bitterly, not Emma. Then I felt ashamed. No matter what I thought of Emma, it was unfair to compare her to someone long dead and virtually sanctified. I shook my head clear of the image.

"Planning on staying here long?" I finally asked in a jesting tone, as I glanced pointedly around the nearly empty room.

"As long as Lorenza will have me."

"She's not going to fire you. Maybe she should, but she won't."

"Is it fair to say you don't like me, Alice?"

"My personal opinion of you is irrelevant. More to the point, let's just say that Lorenza is a good woman, and I don't want to see a good woman get screwed without her consent."

"I haven't lied to Lorenza."

"But have you told her the whole truth?"

There was a long silence in which any feeling of good companionship between us flowed quickly away through the cracks in the floorboards.

"You obviously think I should have told her something you think I haven't."

"Why don't you start off with what you have told her. If I'm wrong, I owe you an apology."

"Why do I feel like I'm in a poker game and you're just waiting to call my bluff?"

"If you have the cards, you win the game and no bluff is involved." I was scrambling on the card bit. I've never even played Old Maid.

Emma gestured toward my glass and raised her eyebrows.

I shook my head.

"If I don't fill in the details you're looking for, feel free to ask," she said with a wry smile.

"Absolutely." I didn't smile back.

She stretched out in the chair and took a deep breath. "Okay, here goes. When I saw Lorenza's ad for a chef, I sent in my résumé. Along with my education and the jobs I had held, I also said I had owned a restaurant in San Francisco called The Bountiful Harvest, which bombed. Within a week of sending her the résumé, Lorenza called me for an interview. I told her honestly that my place failed because of my inexperience and incompetence in managing an entire operation. She knew about Peters's reviews. I did not blame him for my failure. I told her he had been honest in his assessment. Maybe I didn't like how he said it, but I couldn't quarrel with the conclusions. Despite all that, Lorenza hired me anyway. I may not be able to run a restaurant, but I can cook. I demonstrated that to her satisfaction before I started at The Lovage, and she has been satisfied with my work since. And so, by the way, has Elena."

That last comment was meant to clinch the argument. Emma was no fool. She had obviously figured out that Lorenza might be a soft touch from time to time, but that Elena had zero tolerance for errors if they could have a negative effect on The Lovage. So I assumed Emma was telling me not only that Elena liked her work but also that she was convinced that she, Emma, was innocent of what had gone wrong the night of Peters's death. I decided I better have a private talk with Elena.

"Do you want me to open the windows? It seems to be getting a little warm in here. The breeze from the water should be blowing by now."

Funny she should think I might feel warm. The hair at the back of my neck was drenched with perspiration, and moisture from my forehead was rising quickly at the dam formed by my eyebrows. "It does seem a bit warm, yes." As Emma got up to open the windows, I discretely swept what felt like a cup of accumulated sweat off my brow.

"Have I answered your concerns?" she asked hopefully.

"No question you can cook. I remember some great stuff at The Bountiful Harvest. But after the failure of your restaurant, surely you knew how important it was to be there early the day of Peters's review. You were incredibly late getting there. You said so yourself. Why?"

"Someone slashed three of my tires. I didn't notice until I was ready to come down to The Lovage. It took a while to get AAA out."

How odd. Normally peaceful Livorno had been a veritable den of iniquity that one day: slashed tires, death by favas, a stabbing, and maybe a thwarted burglary.

"Did you tell Thompson about that?"

"I don't remember. Maybe not. It didn't seem important." She bent her head and studied her nails with immense concentration. "Is that it?"

"Not quite. What about Tony Petroni? Why didn't you tell Lorenza you knew Peters's son?"

"I didn't think it was important."

"And you didn't think it was important to add his telephone number or address to your employment papers in case anyone needed to reach him if something happened to you?"

"I must have been interrupted while I was completing the forms, Alice. I really don't remember. Besides, who expects to use that information anyway?"

Something only the young would assume, I thought. "Maybe you didn't want to put anything down because you didn't want anyone to contact him."

"He's my best friend. Why would I do that?"

"For the same strange reason that you haven't contacted him since you disappeared off the face of the earth when your restaurant failed."

Emma spun her face away from me as quickly as if I had just slapped her.

"How did you know that?"

"Tony is working in San Francisco at Walton Square, where I ran into him, and I just had dinner with him and John last night. Interesting stories they had to tell."

"Alice, I haven't been lying to you."

"Maybe not, but pulling the truth out of you is like..."

Emma swung around in her chair, her face reddening with fury. "So you want to hear every miserable, humiliating detail? You want to know what it's like to dream of your own business, work sixteen hours every day, save every penny, finally get what you've always wanted, see it soar, and then watch it crash? You want to know how I went into a drunken stupor for a month after, only going out of my apartment at night to get more booze, tossing all the mail, ignoring all the calls, not even bothering to bathe?"

"Emma..."

"Of course you do! And you want to hear how my landlord got the police to evict me because I wasn't paying my rent and I was damaging his property and annoying the neighbors by smashing bottles against the walls when I went into rages. And you're just dying to hear how it felt to find myself sobering up in an alley, curled up with the garbage, and smelling worse than it did. Hearing all that, I assume, would make you feel like you've finally heard the truth! And justify your suspicion and dislike of me. Well, guess what? I've already told Lorenza the basic outline of all that. Admittedly, I did leave out some details like the kind of garbage and the name of the alley. But even though I don't think it's any of your goddamned business, I will be happy to supply you with any of those missing and very pertinent details."

She was so mad, she was virtually hissing. I could almost see her throwing bottles against the wall in sheer frustrated fury. But the anger was clearly against herself, not me. Then I began to wonder if she had forgiven herself totally yet. Instinctively, I reached out my hand to her, palm up in a gesture of conciliation. "I'm sorry, Emma. I really am. I had no idea."

She fell limply back into the chair, all energy drained and the redness receding quickly from her face. "I shouldn't have gone off on you. You were only trying to protect Lorenza. She deserves that, and you're a good friend to do it, Alice. I envy her."

"I didn't mean to open up old wounds, and I wasn't just curious."

"No, and there's no reason why you shouldn't know the rest." She sighed and sat up again, a little straighter. "I couldn't face Tony, which is why I never called him. I hated his father for telling the truth, and I knew Tony would try to defend me. I didn't want to get between him and his father. I also didn't want to cause any problems between John and Tony. John worshiped Tony's father. They are a bit alike."

"So I suspected."

Emma almost smiled. "I wanted to get myself back together before I got back in touch. It just took longer than I thought. After I woke up in that alley, I went to a homeless shelter, got a shower, some clothes, and a hot meal. To make a long story short, I moved into a Mission Street hotel and worked as a short-order cook in some of the better greasy spoons in San Francisco." She hesitated and then looked me right in the eyes. "And I have verifiable references from every single one of them just in case you think I'm giving you a sob story."

I was the one to blink first.

"I may never get the smell of fatty hamburgers and overripe onions out of my nostrils."

"What about your mother. Couldn't she have helped?"

"I was helping her from the day I got my first paper route and earned any money at all. Tony probably told you she and I aren't close. My dad had a drug problem and lost one job after another until he couldn't face her or himself any more and drove his car off a cliff near Devil's Slide. I was about thirteen. Maybe she could have left him earlier or found some nice guy to take care of her later if she hadn't had me. I always felt I was in the way and we fought a lot."

I nodded.

"Actually, we get along now. It's just taken me some years and some rough spots to realize how hard it was for her. She's made some mistakes, but then so have I. And we've gotten closer. She knows most of what happened. I always sent money to her before I paid the other bills, even my debt on The Bountiful Harvest. I only missed that one month. To her credit, she was more worried about me than the lost payment when I did call her."

How different from my mother's reaction when Frances died. She didn't even come to the funeral. I stared out the window and watched the light flash like sparks off the water in the afternoon sun. "And now? Will you call Tony now?"

"You talked to him, Alice. Did he really want to hear from me after all this time?"

"He does. And I think John may be willing to drop the lawsuit against Lorenza if you can explain what happened the night Peters died. He was the one to push the legal thing, not Tony."

"I didn't think that was Tony's style. But what does John want me to do? Take the blame so he can sue me instead of Lorenza?"

"Well, I…"

"Not a bad idea, actually." Emma chuckled and gestured at the virtually empty flat. "He'd not get much out of it if he did!"

"Emma, I have to ask this. Did you know Peters was allergic to fava beans?" After everything else that had been said, I decided I might as well just come out with it.

"I should have known there was one more detail I hadn't told you." But this time she had a smile, even a warm one.

"And did you know what was in that filling you threw out?"

"*Two* details! Goodness. What else?" But before I could answer, she continued. "Yes, I knew about Peters's allergy. Tony and I virtually grew up in each other's homes. I remember how scared he was when his father was taken to the emergency room. I had no idea about his father's heart problems. Those came after I was no longer in touch. And to answer your second question, I really didn't recognize what that mash was. I do know what favas look like fresh, and I've used them in recipes but not often. Anything else I might have forgotten?"

I opened my mouth to form some kind of stunningly intelligent and pertinent question when the telephone rang. Emma disappeared to answer it.

"It's for you," she shouted. "Lorenza."

I walked into Emma's dark bedroom, sat on her neatly made bed and picked up the phone from the floor. Lorenza should know me better. I wouldn't have shorted her chef. "I delivered everything," I said with mild annoyance.

But Lorenza's voice crackled with temporarily controlled major hysteria: "Alice!"

"What's wrong?" I asked. I turned slightly so I did not have my back completely to Emma, whose shadowy figure stood in the doorway.

"Elena had to go home sick. Major migraine. I have to take over. I need you down here as soon as possible to work the front and phone. Please!"

"Five minutes." I hung up and turned to Emma. "Crisis. The sick stove is well, but Elena is sick. I'm out of here."

"Does Lorenza need me? I'll come."

"When your doctor releases you for full-time work, you can insist Elena get a vacation. Until then, Lorenza doesn't need you collapsing on her too."

"Then I'll use the time to call Tony and do whatever I need to do to get him to drop the lawsuit against Lorenza."

I smiled at her. "Something tells me that will be of far more benefit than coming down to the restaurant tonight."

Emma walked me to the door in silence. "Thank you for what you did last night, Alice," she said as she held open the door for me. "Maybe you don't think much of me, but you did me a great favor in giving me back a dear friend. And maybe I can undo some damage done to Lorenza, who certainly doesn't need this hassle. She promised she wouldn't tell anyone about what I had gone through. She hoped The Lovage would be a good restart for me. She's been too good and understanding."

Of course. Lorenza the Protector. I should have guessed why my friend had said nothing to me about her new chef's past. I turned and looked at Emma. Oddly enough, the tension was gone from around her mouth and eyes. She looked like a tremendous burden had just been lifted from her. I nodded and started down the stairs.

"Although you didn't ask," I heard her say very softly to my retreating back, "I didn't make the burrito mix." And before I could turn around, the door shut quietly but firmly behind me.

CHAPTER 25

SO, THE STOVE stayed fixed, Elena was over her ghastly migraine in a resurrectional three days, and life went back to its normal routine.

Okay, I'll admit it: I was bored. The whole thing with Peters certainly had gotten my blood to circulate for the first time in…Well, I hadn't felt this alive since Frances died, ghoulish as that sounds. And now the good old routine of getting up, doing the commute/job thing, gardening, giving the felines dinner, and almost daily chitchat with Lorenza, which had done me so well for so many years, was feeling a tad monotonous, almost a bit depressing. Everything was falling back into a familiar pattern again, and so, rather regretfully, was I.

Emma was finally pretty much recovered. She was coming in to work full-time most days. We were polite to each other, in a slightly chilly way, on the rare occasions we met at The Lovage. Quite honestly, I rather avoided the kitchen area when I could so I could steer clear of her. I noticed she would find something to do as far from me as possible when I couldn't. Avoidance seemed to be an unspoken agreement between us.

Tony and John dropped the lawsuit. Whatever Emma said, Tony accepted and even called to thank me for reuniting him with his childhood friend. He and I had warmed to each other, and I dropped in at Walton Square more often so we could talk when there were breaks in the rush. John was almost never there when I got off work, for which I was glad. I had not warmed to him, nor, I suspect, had he to me.

Lorenza was obviously satisfied with Emma's story about what happened that night, and so was Elena. It didn't help that I had brought in the bowl with the mix, thinking like everyone else that Lorenza had made it. I couldn't very well insist that someone should have questioned where it had come from if I hadn't myself. No one else on the staff had even seen the bowl before or after I had brought it in, so its origin remained a mystery. Since favas were no longer the basis for a legal matter, the whole issue was conveniently dropped, albeit with strong reminders about always knowing the source of any prepared ingredient. Favas became a nonissue with everyone but me. I was not happy about that but decided I must really be the only one out of step.

Well, inconceivable as this may seem, I was wrong.

CHAPTER 26

IT WAS SATURDAY morning. I use the term *morning* advisedly. By any sensible standard, three A.M. is a time that shouldn't even exist for any average working stiff. It certainly should be banned for anyone of more mature years, like me, who would be reasonably sound asleep. Instead, I found myself sitting straight up in bed with that instrument of the devil, otherwise known as the telephone, clutched to my ear.

"Lorenza, do you have any idea what time it is?"

"Yes, Alice. The safe at the restaurant has been broken into."

"What!"

"We've been robbed. Will you get down here? Detective Thompson wants to talk to you."

"Give me a few minutes."

"I'm down at the restaurant."

"Somehow I'd guessed that," I muttered.

I confess it took me an extra minute or two to dress. Knowing that Thompson was waiting, I needed just a bit more time to make sure my pants matched T-shirt and socks.

DRESSED IN A stunning black and gray executive-striped jacket, white silk blouse and lightweight black slacks, Angel Thompson sat, square-shouldered and cross-legged, directly in front of me. I might have been just a tad groggy from the unreasonable hour, but I was still quite capable of admiring the view of Livorno's finest.

"Nothing missing at all?" my detective asked.

Lorenza shook her head. "Definitely no money. Do you think someone scared them away before they took the cash?"

I looked back at the safe. The door was standing wide open. Even a shortsighted amateur thief with only one eye open couldn't fail to see the bundled bills and rolled coins in plain view. And despite Lorenza's announcement that someone had broken into The Lovage, I saw no obvious signs of forced entry liked smashed doors, broken windows, or blasted safe.

"Maybe," Thompson replied. "But there aren't many people usually around the streets of Livorno at this time of the morning." She waved toward the back door. "The man across the way there said he'd gotten up to go to the bathroom. He saw the lights going on in the kitchen area and knew that wasn't your usual pattern. After the stabbing, he was rather nervous so he called us. He thought he might have seen a silhouette or two, but didn't actually see anyone enter or leave."

"Strange," I said.

"Are you sure nothing looks odd? Anything at all unusual? Were you keeping something else valuable here besides money?" Thompson shifted slightly in her chair.

"Nothing." Lorenza shook her head wearily.

With all these "nothings," this was turning into a burglary that hadn't happened, a figment of the imagination. But it clearly wasn't "nothing." I got up and looked more closely into the safe. There was something missing all right.

"The watch, Lorenza. Did anyone ever claim that watch?"

"What watch?"

"The one some woman lost the night Peters died. You remember, the ugly fake Rolex. I put it into the safe that night. I don't see it."

Lorenza blinked. "I don't think anyone ever claimed it. I'd forgotten all about it."

"Then it should still be there." I pointed at the safe.

"Who knows the combination to the safe?" Thompson asked.

Clearly she thought the thing hadn't been jimmied either. That we were thinking ever so alike gave me just the tiniest little thrill.

"Alice, Emma, and me. Elena worried she'd forget it without keeping a copy of the numbers in her purse, so she didn't even want to know it."

"Alice?"

Thompson flashed one of those wonderful smiles at me. I glowed in return. "I was in bed with my cats from eight until Lorenza called. I'm sure they'll vouch for me if I bribe them with tuna in a light fish sauce."

"Actually, I wasn't asking for an alibi as much as confirmation on who knew the safe combination."

I felt my face flush with embarrassment. "Confirmed," I mumbled.

"And Emma? Was she in tonight and when did she leave?" Thompson was no longer smiling.

"Emma was in tonight and left around eleven. In fact, we walked out together. She wouldn't steal from me. She has no reason," Lorenza said.

Wasn't it interesting that the word theft came immediately to my dear friend's mind when Emma's name was mentioned? Kind of like a mental Rorschach test?

"I wasn't suggesting she had. Maybe she had a good reason to tell someone else on the staff what the combination was?"

Lorenza shook her head.

"Not even Elena?" Thompson asked.

"Elena had it when Emma was recuperating but insisted we change the combination after Emma got back full time. She wanted nothing to do with knowing the combination after that."

"Elena is a brilliant chef but considers herself numerically challenged," I added. "Her ten-year-old granddaughter balances her checkbook for her every week."

Thompson smiled.

"But back to Emma. Even I would agree she wouldn't steal. After all Lorenza has done for her, she certainly has no reason," I said. "And I would have to credit her with more sense than to leave several hundred dollars and take a silly watch instead."

Thompson raised her eyebrows. "You don't like Emma?"

"I don't trust her."

"This is not the time to bring up your unreasonable dislike of my chef," Lorenza snapped.

"And completely irrelevant in this case because no money was taken. Even I think she's innocent, Lorenza. I'm really not accusing her of breaking and entering." Well, maybe I wasn't.

"And what are your reasons for distrusting Emma otherwise?" Thompson was beginning to draw geometric patterns on her notepad.

"Alice came up with some bizarre theory that Emma was responsible for putting uncooked favas in Peters's burrito, thereby causing the allergic reaction which might have set off his heart attack. Emma is no poisoner!"

"Now wait a minute! I never said she poisoned him."

Thompson said nothing. She just looked at me.

"I only suggested that Emma had some explaining to do about that night. And I did think she was somehow responsible for Peters being fed something he was allergic to. In no way did I mean to suggest she deliberately tried to kill him."

"No question of a poison being involved. With his sensitivity to that bean and his weak heart, eating them couldn't have helped, however." Thompson's steady look was making me uncomfortable. I was glad I wasn't one of her suspects.

"Look, that bean mix didn't appear out of thin air. And if she didn't prepare it herself, as she claimed, I still suspect she had something to do with it getting here."

"Why? And even if she did, how would she know he'd order that particular item?" At least Thompson looked curious.

"Exactly!" Lorenza slammed her fist down on the table.

"At least say *ouch*," I grumbled uncomfortably. Her gesture reminded me too much of John's that afternoon at Walton Square when I first met Tony.

"Explain why you think Emma's more likely involved than, say, the dishwasher or a busboy or…"

"I can't explain it. It's just instinct, I guess. But we never did find out where the mix came from, and, oddly enough, Emma tossed it as soon as she heard Peters had keeled over. If nothing else, I find that very interesting behavior."

Thompson raised her eyebrows and nodded encouragingly.

"And she was the owner of a restaurant that closed, at least in part, thanks to two bad reviews from Peters."

"Motive for something?"

"Exactly. And she admitted to me she knew about Peters's allergy from Tony."

"I won't ask when you questioned her." Lorenza was staring at me as if she couldn't decide whether I was just insensitive or grossly insensitive. I suspected she was concluding the latter.

"Tony?"

"Peters's son," I replied to Thompson. "You remember. Antonio Petroni was Peters's son. Tony filed the lawsuit against Lorenza, now dropped thanks to some effort on my part." I shot Lorenza a look that I hoped would remind her I could be a good friend as well as an inconsiderate boor.

"You think he and Emma were involved in feeding Peters the favas?"

"Angel! You can't be taking this nonsense seriously?" Lorenza was virtually sputtering with indignation.

I snorted self-righteously. "Lorenza, Emma had means, motive, and opportunity. And you have to admit her reaction to Peters's death was odd. I'm not making this up just because I've taken some irrational dislike to your cook. I may not be crazy about her, but give me credit for being fair!"

"Usually fair," Lorenza admitted a little more grudgingly than I would have hoped.

Thompson held up her hands.

"We're not fighting," I protested.

"It's just a family feud," Lorenza said at almost the same time.

"All right. So explain to me about Tony and Emma and the fava mix." Thompson was delightfully dogged. She was also taking me seriously, and I liked that.

"I don't think Tony was involved. He told me he hadn't seen Emma since her business went under. And I believe him."

"Instinct again?" she asked.

"Yes. But his father was not a rich man and whatever quarrels they may have had in the past had been resolved. Tony spoke lovingly but objectively about his father and is helping Peters's widowed girlfriend financially. So I can't imagine he needed any money or had any pending grievances. Now, John…"

"John?"

"Tony's significant appendage. He was also Peters's secretary. I think you got the family doctor's name from him. Either you or another police officer questioned him the night Peters died."

"I'll check on that. Meanwhile, what about John?"

"He has a temper, but, to be fair," I emphasized that last word, "he seemed to idolize Peters. In fact, the two are a lot alike." I rolled my eyes heavenward.

Thompson chuckled.

"So it just comes back to Emma," Lorenza said. She did not look pleased. On the other hand, she also didn't look as if she were dismissing my concerns as much as she had before. "But however much you want to blame Emma for the fiasco with Peters, this burglary has nothing whatsoever to do with that. So why even bother to bring it all up?"

"Because I find it a little strange that Peters dropped dead in The Lovage and that Emma was stabbed just outside here the same night. And that very same day, Emma's tires were slashed. I don't think she told you that. And then, not too long after, your restaurant is broken into, Lorenza. We almost have a major crime wave here." I folded my arms and sat straight up in the chair as if this were a well-thought-out theory instead of the spur-of-the-moment inspiration it really was.

Thompson was sitting back in her chair, drawing interconnecting circles on her notepad. She seemed to be ignoring us both.

Lorenza glanced at my detective's artwork. Her eyes widened in shock. "You think all that is connected?"

"Alice may have a point. Think about it. How much crime has there been in Livorno in the last hundred years? Not a lot. Were this San Francisco or Berkeley, I wouldn't wonder about it. Livorno, however, is, well, Livorno."

"Do you think it all has something to do with The Lovage?" Lorenza looked worried.

"I don't know. Do you know of any reason why all this should happen here?"

"No," Lorenza sighed. "I don't. The Lovage is doing well, but I'm not making a lot after expenses yet. There aren't any local competitors who would get more business if I went under." She hesitated. "I really am trying to think ruthless here, and I just can't come up with any reason why anyone would want to do in the restaurant."

"Maybe Emma does." Thompson put down her notepad.

I waited for Lorenza to respond first. She didn't. I thought that was a significant change in her prior defense of her chef.

"Why don't we call her and get her down here?" I finally suggested.

Thompson nodded, and Lorenza headed for the telephone in the front of the restaurant. I said nothing to my dear detective. I just smiled at her, and she smiled back. It was a wonderful moment.

"No one is answering. I just got her answering machine but didn't leave a message. I'll try again later." Lorenza looked at me with a puzzled expression. I nodded. Somehow I suspected we were both thinking it was a little early for Emma to be up and out when she couldn't possibly have been in bed until midnight or later.

But I opted for a reasonable explanation. "Maybe she has the phone turned off. I've done that after some telemarketers woke me up at eight-thirty a few nights running."

"Is she scheduled to come in today?" Thompson asked.

"No. It's her day off."

I looked up at a window and saw the blue-gray light of early morning. "Tell you what. I'll go up to her place and bring her down. It's going to be too hot to sleep much longer anyway." I relished the idea of rousting Emma out of bed, then felt ashamed; I didn't approve of using Gestapo techniques on anyone.

"That's better than me doing it," Thompson replied with a smile. "I don't want her to think I suspect her of anything on this safe cracking...or re-opening, really, but I do feel she just might have a bit more information she hadn't thought to give me before on her stabbing."

"Frankly, I don't know which would scare her more," Lorenza said with a raised eyebrow in my direction. "You waking her in the middle of the night or Alice."

This was one time I thought Lorenza might just be right.

CHAPTER 27

IT WAS NO later than seven A.M. when I finally walked out of The Lovage. The air was motionless and already heating up for what promised to be one hellish day. Despite lots of good coffee, some sweet fresh strawberries, and a veggie omelet with salsa and pan-fried potatoes, which Lorenza just whipped up on the spur of the moment for Thompson and me, I felt like leftover cat food.

I opened my car door. The steering wheel was already hot to the touch. I rolled down the windows and futilely fanned cooler air toward the inside. "Ugh," I said. A useless complaint. Finally, I got in, started the car, touching the wheel with only two fingers, and turned into the main street.

As I started the ascent to Emma's flat, I began to feel a bit guilty about my early morning outburst. Now that both Thompson and Lorenza were taking my concerns seriously, I was feeling less on the defensive. So I guess I could afford to admit, for all my suspicions about Emma's behavior and involvement in Peters's death, I no longer really disliked the woman. Were I to be even more honest, I would have to concede that I even admired her courage in dragging herself out of an abysmal depression after the loss of her restaurant. And Elena's opinion meant something to me too. Tolerant though she might be of many human frailties, my friend did not suffer fools, slouches, whiners, the cruel, or the dishonest gladly—or silently.

WE HAD HAD our talk, Elena and I, about Emma some days ago when I had driven her to Solano County to visit her son, daughter-in-law, and the checkbook-balancing grandchild. As Elena slid into the passenger seat, I felt the air grow heavy with the volcanic heat of her barely concealed wrath.

"So what's wrong?" I asked.

"Little one, the world is crazy. Did you see the news this morning?"

Elena is a news junkie. She reads two local papers, two national news magazines, actually tapes PBS commentator specials, watches CNN and MSNBC, and I've caught her glancing through Lorenza's copy of the *Wall Street Journal* in her spare time. If I need to know what is going on in the world, the two of them will let me know whether I want to or not. This saves me the time to concentrate on the more serious sections of the paper: those dealing with the spirit, nourishment of the whole person, and philosophy. In short, the gardening section, food on Wednesdays, and the comics.

"Missed it. Edward wanted me to tape the Friskies commercial."

Elena gently slapped my arm. "Maybe your cat was wise. I shouldn't have watched it. That poor little girl!"

I knew from experience that I didn't have to say anything when she was on a roll.

"I can't understand what could be in any mother's mind to put paint on her baby's face, dress her up like a miniature woman, and have her strut like a whore in front of adults. Men as well as women! Child modeling, they called it. Ai!"

"And she didn't deserve to get murdered." I had heard the story and it was an ugly one.

"Child model? Dress her like the baby she was! Have her playing little child's games in little child's clothes. That's a child model. But to make her simper and flirt was disgusting. And what does that teach a girl? It teaches her that the only thing she's good for is selling herself. And selling herself to men especially."

"True," I said, merging into the freeway heading to the wine country.

"And when she's no longer pretty? What's she got then, eh?"

I patted my face. "Wrinkles and fat."

"You! But you're right. She thinks she's nothing. Worthless! She hangs herself at thirty!" Elena raised her arms in a gesture of futility, dropped them, and sighed. "My granddaughter is going to know she has a beautiful mind, not just a lovely little face." Then she beamed. "Guess what she wants for Christmas?"

"Not just two front teeth?"

"Her own computer! And my son promised to start teaching her about investments when school starts. He thinks she's got talent."

He should know. He's a successful investment consultant in the wine country. "No kidding! Anyone who could straighten out your checkbook…" I smiled. "And let me guess who's going to buy her that computer." Not that her son and daughter-in-law wouldn't, but Elena insists on grandparent's rights.

"It's important that I do it. I'm the older Latina generation and I want her to know I think women can be strong, brave, and smart too. Just like you and Lorenza and Emma."

"And you, my friend. And you." I patted her arm.

She shrugged modestly but smiled as she looked out at the dark, wooded, heavily leafed grapevines, trellised and stretched in very even rows over the gently rolling hills.

"You like Emma, don't you?" It was my chance, and I grabbed it.

Elena was silent for a bit and then looked at me. "She's a good woman, little one."

"From you, that's a major compliment."

"But you don't think she is?"

"I don't know what to think. Tell me what I'm missing about her."

Elena put her hand over her heart. "I feel it here," she said. "She works hard. She was reliable before the night Peters died, and she's been reliable since she got back. Everyone loves her enthusiasm. She makes work easier for everyone, and she's kind. You know Daryn?"

"The one with the nose ring."

"Nice boy. His girlfriend dumped him. Emma has been helping him through it. She's like Lorenza. She sees we're family, not a staff. She doesn't think about who's executive chef and who's dishwasher."

"No flaws?"

"One."

I raised an eyebrow.

"She works too hard. Doesn't take good enough care of herself. Just like you and Lorenza."

I laughed. I had no reason to push Elena further. She had answered my question when she put her hand over her heart.

THUS MY FRIEND had put her stamp of approval on Emma as a basically decent sort. And unlike Lorenza, whose good heart sometimes got in the way of her head, Elena had X-ray vision when it came to con artists and other major or minor crooks. As a bright child who started working in the fields at ten and was the single mother of her son at fifteen, she'd learned the darker side of people real fast. If it were up to me, I'd put Elena in charge of national security; we'd never have a spy problem again.

So I did some stepping back and reassessing of Emma. Certainly, I saw no desire for revenge in her, nor any tendency to shift blame away from herself. In fact, she seemed almost too willing to take on all the blame for everything without actually admitting to knowing the most crucial information. She had, for example, taken full responsibility for the failure of the salad and claimed a generic fault with the whole evening. Yet she had shown no curiosity about the origin of the fava mix. She acted like someone who knows something but is willing to take the heat for it even if she really herself is innocent.

How odd. Why would she? Could she be protecting someone? But whom? And why?

Tony immediately came to mind. They had virtually grown up together. There was a strong emotional bond there, but I didn't think he was the one she was shielding. He didn't seem to have it in for his father, let alone anyone else, and he hadn't filed the lawsuit against Lorenza either to do in The Lovage or to get Lorenza's small savings account.

John? To be honest, I was beginning to think he was innocent too, if for no other reason than the man lacked any subtlety of thought, speech, or gesture. Banging tables and disliking me just because I was a fat redhead like his mother were not exactly examples of an intricate thought process. That fava mix required more deviousness than he had demonstrated. Maybe designing salad forks required creativity but not that kind of torturous cunning. His flaws were too straightforward even if I hadn't found any virtues in him yet.

But for Emma to take on someone else's guilt like that must mean the person had a very strong emotional claim on her. I can think of few people in my life I'd do that for, and I didn't think I was that unusual.

Suddenly I realized I had arrived at Emma's dead-end street. Even without encouragement, my car had climbed the hill. I made a U-turn and parked in front of the two-flat building, sighing as I thought of the stairs ahead of me. But this had been my idea, after all, and had won a smile from Thompson. With that inspiration, I pulled myself out of the car and headed for the staircase with the determination of Sir Edmund Hillary after Mt. Everest.

AT THE TOP I hesitated, allowing some time to catch my breath, then knocked at the door.

No response.

I rapped louder.

Nothing.

I banged on the door.

Zilch.

"Emma?" I called, then put my ear to the door. There wasn't a sound.

Frustrated, I turned the doorknob.

Silently, slowly, the door swung open.

THE WINDOWS IN the living room were closed, and, with the growing heat of the day, the flat was unbearably hot and stuffy.

"Anyone home? Emma?"

There was no answer.

I was sweating profusely and needed a breeze. I went over to the windows and wound them open as far as possible, feeling just a hint of cool from the shaded air under the tree. Fortunately, my car was parked in a shadow, just behind Emma's white Sentra, which she parked on the street. Only the lower flat came with the narrow garage.

I looked around the room. It looked as empty and neat as it had the day I brought the soup. No dirty glasses or plates. Emma obviously wasn't one for letting things sit if she ate in here.

I walked into the kitchen. Still no sign of life. Although I hadn't spent much time here, my quick glances apparently hadn't missed anything of significance. There wasn't much to miss. The stove and refrigerator were clean and typically old for a rental. No dishwasher. No microwave. Nothing dirty in the sink. (I checked.)

I opened the refrigerator. There was a half bottle of a decent white zinfandel, some nonfat milk, and a few containers of fruited yogurt, two grapefruit, one apple, and three pears. In the recently defrosted freezer, there was one package of frozen spinach—organic. Spartan but disgustingly healthy.

The oven was clean and empty. In the cabinets and drawers, I found even less to get excited over: an economy-size package of blue corn flakes, a few glasses of various sizes and shapes, two nice wine glasses, a bunch of mismatched flatware with equally ill-assorted dishes, and two pots. The Martha Stewart of Livorno, Emma wasn't.

The cookbooks were fun. She had marked several recipes, presumably to try at The Lovage, which had the equipment to make them. I rather liked the sound of Madras split pea croquettes in a spicy tomato sauce.

By this time I had done enough banging and slamming to know that Emma was not in her flat. I had no idea where she had gone or when, but I thought it odd that someone so organized and apparently methodical would leave for the day, knowing it was going to be hot, without watering her herbs. They were lush, hence normally cared for, but the soil in the pots was dusty dry. I took mercy on them and dumped some water in the containers.

Of course I should have left at that point. Normally, I would have. I certainly had no business probing around Emma's things. My mother would have been horrified. But I stayed. And I snooped. I don't know exactly what I expected to find, but I wasn't going to let a chance to find anything that might answer my questions about this woman go by.

Implausible as this may sound, the bathroom was even less thrilling than the kitchen. Emma was obviously not on any regular medication. She did have some pain pills, but the prescription dates coincided with one of her hospital releases. And there was a large bottle of aspirin. Presumably, she either had tension headaches or menstrual cramps. I patted myself on the back for remembering something so long ago, as if any woman could ever forget those years.

The blond hair was real; no bottles of coloring in the medicine chest or under the sink. Emma brushed and flossed her teeth. There was a sturdy comb and brush in a drawer. Neatly folded on racks between the sink and shower were one washcloth, one bath towel, two hand towels, and one mismatched bath mat.

Boring.

I went back to the living room. It yielded nothing much, although I took some time going through the books. Emma was a history buff. I found some loose CDs on the middle shelf. Except one by the Tokyo String Quartet, they were all jazz.

Disgusting.

I must tell Edward.

The hall closet held one raincoat, one short but heavy jacket, and one short but light jacket. Emma was no clotheshorse.

This was a two-bedroom flat. The smaller room was empty except for a bucket, broom, mop, and a vacuum. There was a goodly array of cleaning stuff organized by type in one corner.

Someone had made the closet into a linen cabinet. I found one set of carefully folded sheets and one set of equally neatly folded hand, bath, and wash towels. She didn't have much, but she certainly took good care of what she had. Sighing, I moved on to the other bedroom.

I don't know why I left this room for last. Maybe I felt embarrassed, a little guilty, going into the most private and personal of places. Poking around more public rooms is one thing, but the bedroom is usually someone's sanctuary. Or perhaps I was afraid of what I'd find.

Whatever the reason, I stood for a moment in the door of that room and looked around before I walked in. The single bed was unmade, unusual for someone so neat. I stepped closer. No, it looked like only one person had slept there: one pillow with one indentation. Our Emma was not a restless sleeper.

The closet door was also open. Emma did not have many clothes, but what she did have was carefully put on hangers or folded. All was incredibly neat, except where she had pushed things aside and pulled a sweatshirt out of a pile, not taking time to straighten the stack or pick up the pants hanger from the floor where it had fallen. Emma had been in an unusual rush whenever she had left the flat.

Deep in thought, I walked over to the phone to call Lorenza and Thompson with the news that the bird had flown somewhere. Then I remembered what Lorenza had said about an answering machine. There hadn't been one the last time I was here. Sure enough, a new cordless phone with voice mail capacity was resting on the floor. There was no flashing message light. Presumably nothing new had come in since Emma left.

Idly, I bent down and pressed the message button. The mechanical voice informed me that there was one old, undeleted message. I decided to listen. After a beep, I heard the following: "Emma. I've got to see you. Now. Call me."

There was something in the insistent and almost seductive tone of the woman's voice that caused me to shiver despite the heat.

CHAPTER 28

"NO, I DIDN'T break down the door. It wasn't locked. And she is not in her flat."

I had decided to call Lorenza and Thompson from Emma's. All I wanted to do was shorten the time before I could go home, plunge into a bathtub of ice cubes, and nap there while dreaming of a vacation to Antarctica.

"Yes, her car is parked out front."

I was beginning to pace as much as the small bedroom would permit.

"How would I know if she took a suitcase? Would I even know if she owned such a thing?" I asked innocently.

As Lorenza conferred with Thompson, I sat down on the bed and rummaged idly through a box near the bed. In the absence of a stand, she apparently used it to hold bedside table things. Emma's most recent bedtime reading was a cookbook from a Buddhist monastery, which fluttered with several tags marking interesting recipes, and a biography of Virginia Woolf. I had to give her credit on the latter. I had never been able to get through that one.

"Why don't I leave her a note to call you?" I was getting hotter by the minute and more impatient by the second.

They were still conferring. I poked around the box some more. Under the books, a few handwritten recipes and next to a spare pair of glasses was a small green binder. I picked it up.

"Why don't I leave her a message to call *each* of you as soon as she gets back?"

I looked at the binder. It seemed to be some kind of diary.

"Yes, Lorenza! I will make sure I put the notes where she'll certainly find them: the bed, the shower, and maybe the refrigerator, although I don't think she bothers to eat much…. No, I have not been snooping in her kitchen! How could you suggest that? She's just thin, that's all."

We agreed to notes, and I hung up. Then I opened the binder to the first page and read a bit. I stopped in shock, then read some more. Emma hadn't discarded all of her past life.

The ice-cube bath would have to wait.

WITH EACH SEPARATE entry, the handwriting began fairly legibly, then slowly disintegrated into words and phrases that were completely indecipherable in places. The paper was stained here and there. I smelled it. Definitely wine. Was all this suggestive of an attempt at a kind of boozy therapy?

I should know. Been there. Done that. But I had tossed my own efforts away years ago.

Most of what Emma had written made no sense. It was a virtual word salad. Maybe a psychologist could make something of it, but I couldn't. What was readable, however, was utterly fascinating, and it all centered on the end of The Bountiful Harvest.

It seems our Emma was in love and not solely with food preparation. Unfortunately, she used initials: *P, D, T, J,* and *M.* It wasn't clear which was the object of her passion. By the time she got into the good stuff, all logical reference was lost, and the lover became just a meaningless squiggle or "she."

But the lover was clearly her first. Seems it was love at first sight. Obsessional love, in fact, for Emma, with "nights to remember." She adored the woman's "fragility," her "innocent seductiveness." She so desperately needed Emma to protect her from "the world." She made Emma "feel needed, complete…" Well, I got the idea.

Very sophomoric, I caught myself thinking self-righteously. That was because Emma had written it, not me. Reality check, Alice! Who was I kidding? I had felt much the same way about Frances, who had been my center, my life, my…

I skipped the continuing paean to the beloved and read a bit from the back.

This part dealt with Emma's attempt to understand the woman she was obsessed with. Seems there was a zinger with the perfect lover! She wasn't exactly faithful and she only cheated on Emma with men, but Emma didn't think the woman was bisexual. Pragmatic was the word she used. An interesting term. Manipulative, selfish, immature were the adjectives that came to my mind, but then I'm a firm believer in monogamy.

From what she wrote about the woman's background, I suppose there was reason to feel sorry for the errant one. It seems she'd been a pretty little thing whose mother decided she should be a child model. Wouldn't Elena find that interesting, I thought. But the child appeared to have shown some promise, per Emma. Or maybe per the woman.

Then her mother died. No mention anywhere of a father or any other family. The girl apparently grew into a klutzy teenager, wandering from one foster home to another. No more modeling career. Just after she got hooked up with a gang that was into petty vandalism, but before she slid into drugs and teen pregnancy, a good foster mother took her on and spruced her up with lessons on clothes and makeup. The girl finished high school and was deemed a success. Success, however, evidently meant finding a good sugar daddy to pay your bills while you played with Emma for good times.

I put the binder down and walked into the kitchen for a much-needed glass of water.

What Emma must have gone through emotionally would be my definition of hell, I thought. Argue as I might that Emma had allowed herself to be victimized in this relationship, I still had to give her credit for more resilience than I'd have had in her place. She not only had the guts to pull herself up by the bootstraps when her restaurant went bust but also when a major love affair went wrong at the same time. And this other woman really seemed to get a maxi kick out of trying to jerk her around.

I washed out the glass, dried it, and put it back. Maybe I was invading her privacy, but at least I could be polite and not leave a mess behind too. Then I went back to the bedroom and my reading.

I flipped back to the story about The Bountiful Harvest. Seems the woman was really into jerking Emma's chain about the time Peters came to do his first review. I remember Frances calling what the woman did "the old tease and withhold trick." Emma was a wreck but hanging in there. Then as the review night approached, the woman apparently gave Emma another "night to remember" and promised to help her out, knowing how nervous she must be.

When Emma told her that pasta primavera would be the specialty, the woman told her she had an "in" with Peters, could find out just how he liked it, and would make sure Emma got some of the entrée done precisely to his taste. Totally blinded by the woman, Emma grabbed at the offer and didn't even bother to check when the dish arrived. She just made sure Peters got it. Questionable chef ethics at best and a stupid decision at worst. That night was her first disaster.

But did our Emma wake up? Apparently not. Seems the lover gave the performance of her life, pleaded for forgiveness as she claimed all sorts of mistakes by everyone else except her, then teased and tormented our Emma into a sexual frenzy. She became quite graphic before the entry became unreadable.

My face got hotter than an overheated flat would explain, and I took a couple of minutes to fan myself with the Buddhist monastery cookbook. Then I hurriedly skipped through the diary to the next episode in this lesbian version of a late-night TV soap.

By the time of the second review, Emma was not only physically exhausted by the effort to produce the killer menus needed to regain the customers she'd lost after the first review, she was at an emotional breaking point. This woman's bag of tricks must have made Mata Hari look like a sexual piker. In short, our Emma was in a pretty fragile position psychologically.

Enter the night of Peters's second review. Before he was scheduled to arrive, the woman called Emma at the restaurant, threatening suicide. She was literally sitting at the phone with a fifth of scotch and a bottle of sleeping tablets. It was the guilt she felt over the disaster of the first review, even though it wasn't totally her fault, of course. And she knew Emma couldn't love her any more, could she?

Well, what do you suppose our Emma did? What would I have done? What would anyone have done? She left the restaurant. Understandable. But stupid, stupid, stupid.

It was a rainy Saturday night. There was a large red wine blotch on the page, but I think the woman lived in or near Daly City. By the time Emma got to the apartment, no one answered the door. Apparently, they hadn't traded keys. Emma certainly didn't have one. She tried to get the apartment manager to open the door. He didn't believe the suicide story. By the time he was convinced and opened the apartment door, guess who wasn't even there.

By the time Emma got back, still hoping like a fool that the woman had left a message, the damage had been done. Seems someone had called and told the sous-chef to go home because business was slow, Emma was on her way and could handle it all herself! Several of the staff had been sent home too for the same reason. No one questioned it. Business was pretty bad.

And we all know the results of the second Peters review.

I skimmed through the rest of the material, but there was little of interest. Some mention of a sister and mother. Whose I couldn't figure out. And apparently someone worked downtown at Nordstrom. Maybe *D.* Or was it *P?* I couldn't read the handwriting and gave up. There was no indication that Emma had ever seen the woman again. That was the most intelligent thing she had done for some time!

CHAPTER 29

A SENSIBLE PERSON would have called Detective Thompson, admitted reading the diary, and told her what was in it, just in case she might find it interesting. After all, I was on a credibility roll with her. But then a sensible person would never have gotten involved in this whole mess in the first place. And I just could not admit I had been so slimy as to snoop through Emma's entire flat and then read her most personal stuff. Lorenza would never forgive me. I wasn't sure I could forgive myself. After all, the lawsuit was over. I couldn't see any connection with The Lovage burglary. The diary could remain private.

I stood up. Emma had probably gone somewhere for the day, and Thompson could interview her tomorrow or later today. I stuck the binder back underneath the recipes, found some paper in my purse, and wrote out the promised "please call" notes. Then I left for home.

AS I WALKED through my door, I swore irritably at the oppressive heat in the house. Tonight I wouldn't even need to microwave dinner. It was so hot that all I had to do was put an egg on the counter. In five minutes, it would be perfectly boiled.

Edward and Piers had anticipated me and were lying in the cool bathtub. At least I had the bed to myself. So I lay down, stretched out so each body part was exposed to the hope of any circulating air, and thought.

Guilt I certainly felt for my snooping, but I also felt vindicated.

From what I had seen in Emma's binder, I might not have been all that far off when I thought she was hiding something. Although it appeared that the lover from hell was out of her life and that Emma had pulled herself together, I couldn't help thinking that something from that past had somehow resurrected itself in the fava mix.

I wasn't going to bother Thompson about this. She'd be in touch with Emma soon enough and would be busy with details and reports from the burglary as well as still working on the stabbing. In a moment of wild imagination, I had suggested all three strange events might be connected, and I could easily see where the burglary and the stabbing might be. Emma was in the wrong place at the wrong time. But the favas, the stabbing, and the theft of the watch? Maybe connecting all three was stretching it a bit.

But did I really think the fava mix was unrelated? After all, the purpose of it wasn't clear. The more I thought about it the more I decided Emma knew who had brought the mix and why. And the whole situation had intimations of the two Bountiful Harvest nights. Had that woman really stayed out of Emma's life? Or had she perhaps just dropped back in again?

I reached for the telephone and called Tony.

"John!" I trilled with forced enthusiasm when he, not Tony, answered on the second ring.

"Shit!" I heard him grumble. "Yes, Ma. What can I do for you?"

"It's Alice, not your mother. Alice McDoughall. Do I really sound that much like your mother?" It was bad enough I bore some unforgettable resemblance to the clearly unpleasant woman. I didn't want to sound like her too. I have some pride.

"Al-lice! Of course you don't. Maybe just for a moment there. Certain quality of voice…but never mind. What can I do for you, dear heart?"

My self-control was admirable, especially after being called by Peters's obnoxious endearment. "Actually, I wanted to talk to Tony for just a minute. Is he there?"

"In the bathroom. Tony!"

My ears hurt.

"You want to wait or have him call you back?"

"Well, I had a question about mushrooms." Then I realized that John might have the answer to my question as well as Tony. And if there were any reason to protect Emma, he would be less likely to do it after all the mean things he thought she had done to his beloved. "I'll wait. Haven't had a chance to talk to you for a while anyway!" I chirped cheerfully. I hate it when I lie like that.

To John's credit, he remained silent.

"Seen Emma recently?" It was probably just as well to plunge in immediately.

"Last week. She and Tony have made up. You know the lawsuit is off."

I wasn't sure John was too happy about that from the tone of his voice. "Yes! I'm happy to see good friends back together though."

"Hmm."

"You know, Emma really is a nice person. Is she with someone?"

"She didn't say anything to Tony about that."

"Maybe she's just in between. I thought she had a long-term relationship about the time she owned The Bountiful Harvest."

John hesitated and then yelled, "Hey, Tony! Is Emma shagging anyone? I think Alice wants to ask her out."

No, but I wanted to throw the receiver as far as the cord would allow. Had John been anywhere near, I'd have shoved it down his sweet little throat.

"Alice?"

Tony had picked up the phone.

"I do not want to ask Emma out," I said, trying not to grind my teeth. "I was just telling John I was surprised she wasn't with someone and thought she had said something about a relationship around the time she owned The Bountiful Harvest."

"Not that I know about. John? Did Emma ever mention anyone to you?"

In the background, I heard something like a laugh and then "Not only no, but hell no." Maybe Emma wasn't all that fond of The Appendage either.

"No. I don't know of anyone. Why?"

"No reason. I didn't mean to make a big deal of this. I just think nice people should be with nice people. I'm a romantic."

"You aren't with anyone."

"I'm a widow. That's different." Tony was such a sweetheart!

"Sorry! Has it been long?"

"Several years. It's okay. I've pretty much recovered." Like when hell freezes over.

"You called about something else?"

I hesitated, trying to remember what lie I had told John. "Oh yes. Mushrooms. Morels."

"*Un-huh?*"

"How do you cut them?"

"Any way you want."

"Tony, you're a darling. Thank you! I won't keep you. Give John my best."

And I hung up quickly before he could tell me what a stupid excuse that had been to call him. And now they were both probably thinking I had a thing for Emma. On the other hand, I found it interesting that neither of them knew anything about Emma's very passionate attachment.

CHAPTER 30

SUNDAY WAS TOO hot to even remember. After another blistering hot night during which the cats slept in the bathtub and I wished I had, I was not ready for work the next day. For the hundredth time, I swore I would put in air conditioning. I was getting too old for nights like these.

But I got up, showered, tried to dry, gave up, and threw on something loose. Normally, I'm a breakfast person. I passed on everything except a glass of iced tea. Once I got into the city, I'd pick up something. It might even be cool enough to eat there. Then it was time to leave. Fortunately for both the insurance industry and us, my car got us safely to work with minimal assistance from me.

There is no way you can slip into an office unnoticed. I suppose it's possible in big ones, but, with my luck, I'd fail there too. So, with iced cappuccino, a double orange juice, and scrambled eggs on a sesame bagel in hand, I wended my way through all those coworkers who were just beaming with joy over the great weather while I smiled cheerily and hoped I had some aspirin in my desk.

I didn't, but my message light was blinking wearily, and my in-basket had grown six inches since Friday. I opted to ignore everything. Picking up my bagel, I was just about to take a nice soothing bite when my boss walked in with a scowl on his face and the daily schedule of meetings rattling in his hand. When would he learn e-mail and why did I think this was not going to be a good day?

The meetings could have been worse, I suppose. After all, by the time you mentally edit out all the currently popular buzzwords, you've cut at least an hour off each one. Then there are the statistical presentations. Since they are usually geared to what the audience of managers wants to hear, you can probably ignore most of the cute little charts and eye-catching graphics. That's good for another hour. The only real problem is that you aren't really cutting anything short.

And then there is the attempt not to fall asleep. If you do, you just might miss the one important and possibly unpleasant fact slipped into all the other shreddable junk. And if you miss that, it could mean your job. I've learned to sleep with my eyes and ears open.

By eleven, I was back in my glass-enclosed hutch. My eggs were cold, and my orange juice was warm. It was nearly lunchtime for us six o'clockers. I tossed breakfast into the trash.

The message light was still blinking. I picked up a pencil, pulled a legal pad out from what had now overflowed from my in-basket, and punched the retrieve button. Most of the messages were easy. They were either answers to questions I had called about or questions I could call back on. With luck, I would get their voice mail and not have to waste time chitchatting. I sighed and hit the button for the next message.

"Alice. Call me. Emma's not been in."

I dialed The Lovage.

Elena answered the phone. "What's this with Emma?," I asked.

"She never showed up for dinner last night. This isn't like her, little one."

Whatever I might think of Emma, I knew she was reliable about work. Even when she was in the hospital, she called Lorenza or Elena about menu ideas. Once she was home, she'd call to ask if she could do something, anything.

"I know," I said.

"You were at her flat. Did you see anything?…"

Elena knows me too well. She assumed I'd looked around. "I did get the impression she'd left in a hurry, but I can't be sure. Maybe her mother got sick suddenly or something?"

"It takes a minute to call and leave us a message. She'd take that minute."

Now I was beginning to get concerned. "Did you or Lorenza call Thompson?"

"No. You think we should?"

"Maybe. And maybe Emma'll call later."

"Maybe we'll wait until the dinner shift tonight. If she hasn't called by then, we'll call your detective."

My detective? I wish!

I hung up but started to tap my pencil nervously on the pad.

I was worried.

I HAVE ALWAYS been amazed at the efficiency of the subconscious. Sometimes I mentally file stuff away, then some strange little fact comes bursting out, often years later, when I need it but have forgotten totally that I even knew it. And sometimes this happens when I least expect it and occasionally when it is not exactly convenient.

So it was on my last call of the morning. After talking to Elena, I started returning my messages. Some I lucked out on. I could leave a voice mail response. Of course the one person I thought most personified the term *pompous ass* answered his phone. As he went off on his usual long-winded pitch, which was probably an almost-verbatim quote out of the latest management best-seller, I began drawing stick figures with halos.

I was right in the middle of muttering some warm and fuzzy *un-huh* when my subconscious hit me with a delivery.

"That's it!" I said out loud.

"I knew I could finally get you to see it. It's so obvious if you just stop and think about it." The voice at the other end was ever so smug.

"Yes, it is," I said with genuine enthusiasm. "Tell you what. I'll pass your thoughts along to my boss and call you back with any questions or concerns. We really appreciate your input!" And I hung up before I got chapter six of whatever book he was reading.

IT WAS LONG past my lunchtime, but the thought of eating did not appeal after a hot, sleepless night. For once food was not the reason I was out the door, down the stairs, and onto the street in two fast minutes. Despite the smell of today's fresh exhaust fumes mixed with last night's garbage and urine burning my lungs, I almost ran, taking shortcuts through alleys to Fifth and Market.

Nordstrom is one of Lorenza's favorite places to shop. To begin with, it was the first major store in San Francisco not to blink at her mention of a size eleven narrow shoe. Bless the Nordstrom wives and their friends who helped bring sanity to the shoe business long before the store expanded into apparel! And once Lorenza succeeded in dragging me there, I became a fan too. As I may have suggested, I am not crazy about your average department store for 222 good reasons. Nordstrom won me over, however, when I found ample women helping ample women find nice clothes in a department not hidden away in the corner of a badly lighted basement. I appreciated their easy blend of commercial realism and grace. I even got a store credit card.

And it was that credit card bill which gave me an excuse to head for their San Francisco Centre store. Of course I could pay it by mail, but I had a reason for wanting to do it personally. The reason involved a certain tall blonde with high heels, short skirt, and opaque sunglasses I had seen, just opposite Emma's flat, on the day I delivered soup.

That tiny bit of information—her license plate—had flipped into my head during the conversation with that client. NORDAMI had nothing to do with Nordic ancestry after all. It was every shopaholic's cry: "Nordstrom's Am I!"

How could I have been so stupid? John's former dinner date had to be Emma's ex-lover. She was clearly a former model, albeit child. A clothes' horse, if I ever saw one. The high-pitched voice was childish. Maybe childlike and innocent to someone blinded by passion like Emma, but I guess I could see the comparison. And what was this woman doing at Emma's flat that day? And what was her connection with the fava beans? And did she now have Emma happily stashed away, exhausted from an enthusiastic reunion, in a cozy double bed in her apartment? I decided it was time to find all of this out.

CHAPTER 31

I WAS WINDING my way up that infernal circular escalator to the main store and on to Customer Service when I saw her out of the corner of my eye. It had to be her: same haircut and color, same long legs partially covered in a short skirt. There she was, on the floor below me, carrying a dress and seemingly matching it to shoes in the shoe department. But no purse. Maybe she worked there?

Unfortunately, I was also losing her as quickly as I had found her. There I was, stuck on the escalator as she was disappearing out of the shoe department on the floor I had just left. Not being a teen-ager anymore and faced with a male mega-Goth on the stair behind me, I opted not to try running down the up escalator. However, looking at the credit card in my hand, I suddenly came up with an idea even Lorenza might consider brilliant. Smiling, I continued on to Customer Service.

THE WOMAN WHO came to help me was pleasant looking and, despite her beautifully colored gray hair, of indeterminate age. I just hoped she was older than I. The helpless look I was practicing might not work on a Gen Xer.

I smiled.

She smiled.

"May I help you?" she asked politely, her voice a pleasing alto.

"I do need help," I said. "You see, I bought a dress last week from an absolutely lovely young woman. She was so helpful, but now I feel I need some jewelry to go with it. I wanted to ask her help."

The polite lady of indeterminate age waited for the proverbial other shoe to drop.

"I can't remember her name." I didn't want her to wait too long and lose patience.

"Do you have the sales slip?"

"I lost it."

"In which department did you buy the dress?"

"I don't remember."

"Was it Encore?" she asked, discretely looking down at my feet.

"The dress wasn't for me," I said, just a tad too quickly.

A look of "why me?" crossed her face.

"You see, she was in the shoe department with this lovely dress, and I was so taken by it that I stopped her and asked whether she had it in my cousin's size."

Even I knew this was a wild story, but I was betting she had been in retail long enough to have heard them all.

She apparently had. She didn't even blink. That was good.

On the other hand, I also guessed she had been in San Francisco long enough to know that thwarted and hostile ex-lovers aren't always of the opposite gender. She was giving me a thorough once-over. That was not good, but I was lucky; she must have decided I probably didn't have a 9mm hidden in my cleavage because she finally smiled.

"You say you found her in the shoe department with a dress?"

"Yes," I sighed, grateful I was coming through as just your average airhead.

"Looking for shoes to go with the dress perhaps?" She was clearly taking this slowly for the ditsy customer, although her tone was excruciatingly polite.

"Oh, yes! She'd just picked up these wonderful pumps with sequins…"

I may have gone an inch too far. It was almost imperceptible, but the polite lady winced.

"Could you describe her?"

"Young." I smiled and shrugged like an elderly grandmother for whom the whole world is young, perhaps with too few exceptions. "Tall. Blonde. Very thin. Dresses…well, like all these young girls do." I was beginning to simper. It was time to stop before I really did go over the edge into the overstated.

"That may be one of our personal shoppers. Didi Whitcomb."

"Dye-Dye?" I was so horrified by the name, I almost slipped out of character, dropping my voice by at least an octave. "Oh, Dyedye!" I squeaked quickly. "Of course! You are such a darling to help. Thank you. Thank you." I reached out and squeezed the polite lady's hand. She didn't look like she felt darling at all, but she did look relieved and even squeezed back in gratitude.

I bounded off with an enthusiasm I hoped the woman would not misunderstand.

"DIDI. YES, I did say I wanted to see Didi Whitcomb." I was being ever so sweet to the woman sitting at the Personal Shopper's desk.

"You have an appointment?" She started to look at her book.

"Of course," I said quickly, staring over her head with such majestic certainty of social position that even the Queen of England would have been impressed.

The woman blinked. "I'll get her."

And she did.

Even without the opaque sunglasses, I recognized her. She was definitely the woman Lorenza had kindly led off in shock the night Peters died, and she was the woman I had seen in front of Emma's flat.

"Your name?" she asked, sitting down as the other woman walked off.

"I'm a friend of Emma Stilwell's," I said, bending over her. "Perhaps we'd best do lunch."

CHAPTER 32

"I COULD GET fired for this," Didi Whitcomb said nervously after taking a healthy bite out of her ploughman's lunch.

"I'm buying you lunch while we talk fashion," I snarled over my salad of mixed veggies with nonfat ranch dressing, hating her youthful metabolism. "I'm not buying you."

She sputtered on her pickled onion.

"Don't choke. Just kidding."

"You aren't funny."

"You aren't the first to make that observation. By the way, is Didi your real first name?"

"It's Dido, actually, but I had a sister just a couple of years older who couldn't pronounce..."

"And Dido became Dye-dye."

"It stuck."

"Could've been worse." My smile was genuine. Lorenza's older sister calls her "Baby." I made a note to remind her of that fact the next time she pissed me off.

"I shouldn't be talking to you." But she relaxed just a bit and took a hefty bite of the Cheshire cheese. My stomach growled out of sheer gastronomical jealousy.

"Look, all I'm trying to do is help Emma out. Her employer is trying to find her and is madder than hell. I'm sure it is all a big misunderstanding and Emma just forgot to tell her she wasn't coming in to work for a bit, but..."

"And you think I should care?"

Ah, so there had been a break in their relationship! I mentally patted myself on the back.

"I picked up Emma's messages. You'd called her."

"You're kidding, of course."

"No. Look, I said I was just a friend. Emma has me water her herbs, check her mail and her messages when she isn't around. Picking up her voice mail isn't unusual..."

"I mean, like why would I call?"

She was beginning to annoy me with the obtuse ploy. "Like for the same reason you came to visit her once, and, like when you saw me, you pretended you were like lost."

"People your age shouldn't try to use in jargon. You get it wrong and sound silly."

I wanted to shove a sourdough roll down her throat. "And maybe you should listen and answer the question asked. You missed the point."

"Didn't miss the point at all, lady. Tell me why I should trust you, and, even if I did, why I should answer your stupid question? How do I know you aren't a nut who's going to go postal on me for no reason?"

Didi did have a point. I shoved the aforementioned roll into my own mouth so I could grind on it instead of on my teeth. It was calming.

I sighed. "Fair enough. But, I repeat, I'm just trying to help Emma and find her so she can call L—er, her boss before she gets in trouble." I slathered butter on the rest of the roll. To hell with calories; I needed fuel.

"The woman in Livorno that day was really you? Hey, what kinda hair color do you use? It's good. Looks real."

I shut my eyes and counted to ten. "It is real. And, yes, it was me."

"Amazing!"

I raised one eyebrow.

"You aren't gray yet?"

I shook my head, not trusting myself to say anything civil.

"Jesus! I turned gray at twenty-seven and it costs me a mint to get this blond right!"

She had really gotten me. I licked my finger, gave her one point in the air, and smiled.

"Okay, lady. I did go to see your friend, but I don't think you want to hear why."

"Test me."

"Look, I'm not your stereotypical dumber-than-dirt blonde. Your being a friend of Emma Stilwell's is no recommendation to me. In fact, that is one very good reason not to trust you at all."

"I'm not trying to get involved in your personal life. I just want to know where Emma is." I had obviously taken the wrong approach with this woman. I opted for a quick counter move. "Maybe {I}friend{/I} is the wrong term. I've only known her for a couple of months, but she works for someone who is a real buddy and is worried that she hasn't shown up for work and hasn't called. Emma seemed nice enough, so I've helped out from time to time. Am I wrong about her? Is there something her boss should know?"

"You think I'll trust you more when you change your story?"

"You want to call Lorenza Galli at The Lovage and verify I'm not an axe murderer?" I threw my hands up in frustration. Didi wasn't stupid, and I was a failure at Basic Suspect Questioning 101.

Didi was looking at me with intense concentration. Then she shook her hair from side to side. It flowed without mussing. Not a cheap haircut. "Okay, I trust you. What do you really want?"

"Where's Emma?"

"Don't know and don't care. She's a pervert."

"A what?"

"P-e-r-v-e-r-t. Sex pervert. She made Jo sick too. And Jo had more reason than I did. Emma made passes at her. Gross! Makes me sick just thinking about it. Woman doing it with a woman. Know what I mean?"

I decided this was not the time to out myself. I coughed.

"Yeah, now you get it. Enough to make you toss your salad."

"Emma was trying to seduce Jo? You saw this?" Tossing my salad over the idea of lesbian sex wasn't exactly on my agenda, but I didn't say that.

"Jo told me about it. I guess they met at some party that Tony, Mr. Peters's son, threw. Not too sure, but it isn't important. Jo said she'd never let Emma near me; the dyke was that gross."

"And Emma never took no for an answer? I thought that was a little unusual for, ah…" I just couldn't bring myself to use the pejorative. That was more acting than I could handle.

"Boy, are you wrong! Jo says sex perverts never back off. They're crazy."

It was my turn to study Didi. Was she lying? Was she trying to hide their relationship? Was she telling the truth, and was Emma really some kind of nut? Who was telling the truth?

Quickly, I weighed the options. Didi may not have been the nicest person I had ever met, but I didn't see her as a psychopath. And even though I wavered back and forth in my opinion of Emma, she had shown every indication of basic stability except on the night of Peters's death. I weighed my impressions and made a decision, which should never have been made by a psychological layman. As they say in ads, don't try this at home. I ignored the advice.

"If Jo didn't want you near Emma and neither of you trusted her not to rape you, given half a chance, why did you go to see her alone that day?"

"It was pretty stupid, but she had been making threats against Jo. I wanted to tell her to stop."

"Threats?"

"First, she said she'd tell Mr. Peters that they were having an affair if Jo didn't—well, you know, do it with her." She swallowed audibly.

"But Peters was dead when you went to see her. His death should have been the end of any threats."

"Then she told Jo she'd make sure the police thought she had something to do with his death if she didn't screw…Yuck!" Another shake of the head.

"Jo told you this too?"

"Sure."

"But you knew where Emma lived?"

"I called directory assistance. I figured she was living close to that restaurant. She didn't have an unlisted number or anything. And I went to warn her off."

"Did you ever see her?"

"No. I realized in time how stupid it was to confront a nut like that alone. And my boyfriend's out of town. I wasn't sure I even wanted him involved. So I wrote her a note instead the next day and mailed it, no return address."

"And did she ever answer you?"

"Oh, yeah. Just what you'd expect too. She called and claimed she'd never done any of those things."

I remembered Emma that day I had seen Didi on the hill. I remembered how pale and weak she'd been. Somehow I couldn't imagine anyone less of a threat to someone's virginity than Emma Stilwell. Nor could I see her as a blackmailer for sexual purposes. Certainly that diary had not been written for public view, and the victim had been Emma, not vice versa. Of course, she could have been imagining the whole thing, but I couldn't see any other evidence to support that conclusion.

"By the way, did Jo ever mention that Emma had threatened Peters? I mean, beyond telling him that she and Jo were sleeping together?"

Didi blinked. "No. Not that I know of. Why?"

"Just curious. Wanted to know how much of a nutcase she was."

"Bad enough, let me tell you. Jo didn't even want me to come with Mr. Peters on those dinner parties anymore."

"Why?'

"Emma had gotten Jo so upset, she was a nervous wreck. I'd

never seen her so much on edge. Jo told me she was afraid Emma would attack me as well as her. She said it was dangerous for us even to be seen together."

There was something here, apart from this whole story, of course, that just wasn't making any sense. For someone who was just a friend, Jo seemed awfully protective of Didi and vice versa. And Jo seemed to have a lot of say in Didi's personal life.

"Why did you go anyway, if Jo didn't want you to?"

"Mr. Peters wanted me there. He knew Jo was upset. She wouldn't tell him why, wouldn't let me either, and he thought she'd relax and enjoy things more if I was there."

"I'm sure he was right. Anyway, do you know where Emma is?"

"No."

"Would Jo know?"

"Look, Jo doesn't need to be bothered by this. Even if she knew where the dyke was, I wouldn't give you her address or phone number. I've put up with this long enough myself. I have to get back to work." She reached for her purse.

I shook my head. "I invited you to lunch, and I said I'd pay. That was the deal." I wasn't going to get any further with Didi. I'd been wrong. She wasn't Emma's grand passion. I had failed miserably. I'd tried to pour honey over the wrong fly.

"That's nice of you, despite your not getting what you wanted," Didi said a little grudgingly. "You do seem pretty straight."

I winced mentally. "It's all right. You're a good friend to Jo…"

"I'm not her friend," Didi said with some indignation.

"But I thought…"

"I'm her sister."

DIDI ABSOLUTELY REFUSED to give me her sister's address. Even an offer of chocolate mousse cheesecake didn't melt her resolve. Despite her rather grudging conclusion that I might be a decent sort after all, she made it abundantly clear that she really did not know me and was totally convinced Emma was a major threat to her sister's virtue. She wasn't about to chance making a judgment error and getting her sister into trouble. Even the argument that I might actually be able to save her sister from a fate worse than death didn't get me anywhere. Didi quite reasonably said she would warn Jo herself. I couldn't blame her. Had this been my sister, I'd have been just as protective.

Her attitude was touching. While we were waiting for the check, Didi told me that they had been sent to separate foster homes when their mother died and had been out of touch for several years. Then Jo showed up one day in need of a personal shopper and got Didi. Jo was using her foster family's last name. Anyway, after having lost her older sister once, she wasn't about to do so again. She really loved Jo.

"I always looked up to her when I was a kid," Didi said as we got up from the table. "She was the pretty one, the talented one."

"Don't cut yourself short." I tucked a hefty tip discretely under my plate. The server had been incredibly nice despite our slowness over lunch. She had probably lost another customer because of us.

"No, really. Mother was pushing her into a modeling career."

"Do tell!" I said, absolutely joyous. "You must tell me all about this while I walk you back to work."

CHAPTER 33

ONE OF THESE days, I will get a cell phone. I have gone from finding them an unnecessary intrusion into what little privacy we've got left to looking at them as a rather handy thing to have—on rare occasions, of course. This, however, was one of those rare occasions. I had finally found a pay phone and was trying to read my address book while fishing money out of my purse, at the same time clutching the greasy receiver to my ear and watching for purse snatchers. It was not a happy experience.

"The Lovage. How may I help you?"

"Heard from Emma yet, Lorenza?"

"Alice! I tried to call you at work. They said you hadn't gotten back from lunch. I was worried."

"Long lines. I'm on my way back. Just thought I'd check in. What about Emma?"

"Nothing. This isn't like her."

"Don't die of shock, but I don't think it is either. I think you better call Thompson. She should know about this. And I'll call Tony. He may know where she is. Maybe Emma's even talked to him today."

"Do that before I call Thompson. Maybe this was just miscommunication and nothing at all sinister."

"Okay. I'll call you back."

And then there is a phone card. That might have been useful too. But I'm either at work or at home when I make calls. Why on earth would I need either a cell phone or a card?

To make life easier right now, I answered myself as I rummaged through the maw of my purse for the change I had accidentally dropped into it during the last call. Hopefully, Tony would be at work. I really didn't want to talk to John again.

Of course he was working, and I was told he was too busy to take a call. It was still the height of lunchtime, which I should have known, and I really didn't want to make an issue of this with the receptionist. It was also the one time I didn't want to leave a message either. I bit my lip and called his house.

"It's Alice, not your mother." John had only just said hello, and I didn't even give him the chance to guess wrong.

"I knew that!"

I'll just bet you did.

"Say, have you or Tony heard from Emma today?"

"Why?"

Why don't you just answer my question, I snarled to myself.

"Lorenza wanted to call her. She's not at home. We thought she might be with Jo." I was pleased with my quick thought on that one.

"No, she hasn't called us. But why would she be with Jo?"

This was beginning to feel like playing twenty questions.

"I just ran into her sister, Didi. She said they might be together."

"Okay, so why call here?"

Until now, I had always felt accountants were rather nice people, especially at tax time. I was beginning to find one rather major exception to that assessment. "Didn't have a chance to ask her for Jo's address. Didi's boss was standing right there." Fortunately, I'm not religious or I'd know I was bound for hell with all the lies I'd told today.

"Okay so her phone number is…"

"I need her address."

"Why? You said your friend wanted to call her."

I put my head back, opened my mouth wide and did a silent scream. The man in the next phone booth looked at me with a startled expression, hurriedly hung up, and scampered away, glancing nervously over his shoulder at me.

"Oh, did I? Sorry. I meant she wanted me to deliver something to her. It's really important, John. Emma's got to get it right away."

And don't ask me why!

He didn't. He even gave me Jo's address. And I thanked him very profusely. My mother would have been proud.

I WAS REALLY late going back to work anyway, so I called my boss, left a message on his voice mail that I had gotten sick over some plastic-encased salad dressing, and picked up my car from the company lot. If he called me at home to confirm I hadn't gone to the baseball game or something, tough. Tomorrow I'd deal with his suspicious questions about my ability to drive all the way back to Livorno with food poisoning. Never mind that I had always managed to come down with the "'flu and other ailments" either on long weekends or my vacations, he always believed anyone claiming to be sick was just out to cheat the company. Made me feel happy that I was doing just that for the first time in over twenty years.

On the other hand, I really wasn't well—mentally. Had I been totally rational, I might have called Lorenza back, told her no one had heard from Emma, and asked her to tell Thompson. Had I been semirational, I might have called the police here and told them to check out a missing person at Jo's address. But somehow I had it in the back of my mind that no adult was considered missing for thirty-six hours, and I couldn't have conveyed sufficient alarm to convince the local cops to knock on the door of an otherwise presumably peaceful citizen. I didn't think "an uneasy feeling" would take lots of priority over a live bank robbery or a fresh corpse in an alley.

Call Thompson? What could she do way out in Livorno? I rather doubt she would "just run over" even if she believed me, and maybe she even would, but the red tape of jurisdiction was probably horrendous. And how serious could I possibly make this sound anyway? Emma was going to see an ex-girlfriend. They might be having a discussion over favas. Wow! I couldn't prove Jo had anything to do with those little beans, and Emma's sex life was none of my business.

So why was I going out to Jo's apartment? Because I was worried. And it didn't take a search warrant, five layers of police bureaucracy, and a potentially explosive public relations disaster for one private citizen to go visit another private citizen to settle what was probably an embarrassing private problem.

I HEADED OUT Geary to Park Presidio through Golden Gate Park and down Nineteenth Avenue. It was the long way around to Daly City, but freeway traffic jams have begun earlier and earlier. I decided it was faster to go by surface streets. For once I was lucky on the lights, and as I drove, I talked myself through what I was going to say I was doing at Jo's door and why. After what Didi had told me about their mutual homophobia, I didn't want Jo to call the vice squad on me.

Maybe I didn't have a video of them "doing it" together, but it looked like Jo was the woman who'd wiped Emma all over the emotional parking lot. The modeling career as a child and the mother's death matched. And Jo was certainly in a position to know when Peters would show up for a review as well as know his food allergy. She might even have been able to wheedle him into a particular choice on the menu. And God knows I'd seen her in action; she was a master wheedler. It was all falling neatly into place.

But Emma was hardly my idea of a wild lesbian rapist; and my dislike of her was primarily based on the legal trouble she had almost gotten Lorenza into. Other than that, she had gained the professional respect of both Lorenza and Elena. And frankly, I admired the courage of anyone who had reached for success in a creative endeavor, touched the top, fallen like Icarus, groveled in literal toxic sludge, picked herself up, and gone on. That spoke volumes about her character. And as far as the lawsuit was concerned, as soon as she found out about it, she took responsibility. This is not the portrait of your average out-of-control sex pervert.

So what game was Jo playing with her sister? I was sure she didn't want Peters to know she was sleeping with Emma as well as with him. That was understandable, but the story she made up required just a bit of a stretch for those of us who know better than to think all lesbians become The Lavender Menace when faced with anything in a metaphorical skirt. To put it bluntly, Jo was the one who didn't seem wrapped all that tightly, not Emma, and she was a master con artist.

DALY CITY IS not a memorable place. It had its fifteen minutes of fame in the '60s after someone did a pop song about houses built of ticky-tacky. The image was a little unfair, although the view of the town from the southern side of Twin Peaks tends to support the idea rather strongly. But it's hard being a small town next to a city with the personality of San Francisco. Even Oakland struggles with that problem, and Gertrude Stein immortalized Oakland.

Anyway, like most people who have spent the major part of their lives in or near San Francisco, I have probably been to Daly City four or five times at most. I needed a map to find Jo's apartment. All the apartments seemed to be sand colored, but I finally found the right one. There weren't many very tall buildings, but hers was a few stories high. And I even found a parking place within a block. Now that's something you'd never find in San Francisco.

The apartment complex looked like it had been built many years ago. Although there was no grass in the front, it looked adequately maintained overall. A small bed of somewhat underwatered flowers was wedged between the sidewalk and the tan stucco walls. To the left of the entrance was a narrow cement driveway that led to a row of stalls for parked cars. Most of the tenants must be working; there were few cars in the slots.

There was no metal security gate at the entrance to the building. That surprised me. But the front door was locked. I glanced at the list of names. Each apartment had a buzzer. There was no Jo and no Peters. I opened my purse and began digging around for the paper with the address on it.

"That's okay," I heard a voice say behind me. "I've got my key."

I turned around and saw a young man in shorts and a Giants T-shirt with a six-pack of Miller Draft in one hand and a key in the other.

"Oh, thank you!" I said, rattling my key ring for veracity and smiling sweetly. "We do have such a problem with our purses!"

I might have been Aunt Minnie the ax murderess, but he cheerfully unlocked the door and let me walk in ahead of him. I weighed my sense of gratitude against my irritation at the stereotypical assumption that a middle-aged woman of significant poundage is of no moment, positively or negatively.

I opted for gratitude.

"Which floor?" he asked as we got into the elevator.

There were buttons on both sides of the elevator. I could have just as easily punched the floor myself, but I didn't think this was the occasion to declare my independence since I was not a resident and the resident I wanted to see probably wouldn't have let me in anyway.

"Top," I simpered, hoping he'd get off before I did.

He did. I was so grateful that I smiled at him in a grandmotherly fashion. Then I quickly pulled out the paper with Jo's address on it. As luck would have it, I really did need the top floor.

The hall off the elevator looked like it belonged in an economy hotel: long, narrow, and sloppily carpeted in a very worn and institutional green. The walls were as tan as the outside and not marked up too badly. The apartment doors looked like varnished plywood—cheap, but each one had a peephole, and the building had obviously made it through the Loma Prieta earthquake, which is more than some expensive housing in San Francisco's Marina District had. Maybe there was rock under the structure.

Jo's place was about halfway down an offshoot hall that seemed to run parallel with the front of the complex. I couldn't resist pushing on the door. It gave a bit. Great security feature, that door! Then I rang the buzzer.

Silence.

I waited.

I rang again.

Nothing.

I put my ear up against the door. At first, I couldn't hear anything. No TV. No radio or stereo. No voices. But then there was something. I couldn't quite tell what it was. Something like a scraping noise on a hardwood floor. It stopped and then started again. It was strange, and I didn't like it.

Of course I could have turned around and left. That's what most people would have done. But now I had convinced myself that Emma was there, and instinct told me that the reason she was there would put the final piece into the puzzle of what happened the night Peters died. Like a dog with a bone, I wasn't going to let go.

CHAPTER 34

"LADY, YOU'RE CRAZIER than a hoot owl! Get out'a here before I call the cops."

The landlord was staring at me, that is if one eye could stare. He'd only cracked his door as much as three chain locks would allow. I could just see his left eye, a watery blue. His accent was from somewhere west of the South.

I puffed myself up to look as powerful as possible and glared intently at his wavering eye. "If you don't let me into that place, I'll ram all of me into that flimsy excuse for a door you have hanging on that apartment. And after I shatter it into compost, every one of your tenants will sue you for not giving them adequate protection against robbers, murderers, and crazies like me."

"Letting you in is illegal."

"So are those doors." I hoped there either really was some requirement in the building code or he thought I knew something he didn't.

His one eye blinked. Then I heard some keys clank.

I'd won.

BULLYING IS NEW to me, but why quarrel with success? I let the poor man, who probably weighted 120 pounds soaking wet, precede me down the hall from his first-floor apartment toward the elevator. He kept looking over his shoulder at me. By the time we got into the elevator, he was actually sweating. Maybe he thought I might pulverize him instead of the door. I smiled at him. He scampered away from me as soon as the elevator door opened on Jo's floor.

When we got to the apartment, he unlocked it.

I stepped in and turned to thank him—manners not to be totally forgotten even under the circumstances—but he was scurrying away from me as fast as he could. I rather wished I could've apologized to him. He was only doing his job after all.

The apartment was hot, stuffy, and absolutely quiet except for vague street noises. The entrance hall was rectangular, uncarpeted, and with a kitchen off to the left. I could see a refrigerator. I assumed there were rooms off to the right, but the doors to them were shut.

"Anyone home?" I sang out. "Jo? Emma?"

Then I heard the noise again, louder. It was definitely a scraping sound from one of the rooms to my right.

Cautiously, I opened one of the doors. The room was sparsely furnished. Maybe a living room. No one was there.

I walked to the other door and slowly swung it open. The room was dark, and the air smelled rancid, like sweat and unwashed underwear. As my eyes adjusted, I could see the curtains were drawn shut, clothes were scattered on the uncarpeted floor, and the bed was unmade. Looking around the door, I saw a chair next to the bedstead. In it, tied and gagged, was Emma.

AS SOON AS she saw me, Emma's eyes grew large, and she began to shake the chair frantically. This was clearly the noise I had heard outside.

"Just a second," I said, rushing to her.

The ropes weren't too hard, but I had to hunt down scissors for the gag. When I finished, she literally fell into my arms and cried.

"Let's get out of here," I said, lifting her back into the chair.

"Alice, I can't move. My legs are numb. For god's sake, get me some water."

I didn't ask questions. I rushed into the kitchen and grabbed a glass of water.

"Can you hold the glass?" She shook her head. I held the glass for her. "Drink slowly." After she'd had a few sips, I pulled the glass back. "What happened?"

"Jo tried to kill me. I haven't had anything to eat or drink since dinner Friday. And this room was so hot…"

"I'm calling the police."

"No phone here. Jo has a cell phone. Do you have a cell?"

I shook my head. "Where's Jo?'

"She said she was going to work this morning. I don't know where that is."

"Can you walk?"

"I'm shaking, but I think I'll be able to move in a few minutes. I'm beginning to feel my legs and feet. You'll have to help me though."

"No problem, but maybe something for your stomach would help the shakes. I'll check the kitchen fast."

Jo obviously wasn't much of a cook. The refrigerator needed defrosting, and I didn't want to think about the age of the one frozen dinner I saw jammed in the freezer. There was a bottle of cheap wine, some bread with a few green spots on it, and jam I didn't even bother to check out. Finally, I found some unopened crackers. I cautiously nibbled one corner. They seemed edible.

"Slowly! Eat slowly." Somewhere I remembered reading that eating or drinking too much or too quickly after a long fast was not a good idea. I opted for caution. I didn't have time to research this.

Emma smiled, patted my arm reassuringly, and slowed down, showing far more self-discipline than I ever would.

"I'll open the windows and get some air in here."

I went over to the curtains, threw them back, and opened the windows as wide as possible. I looked down at the sidewalk below. My car was parked about half a block up the street. A cute little red Miata was starting to park in the space behind it. It shouldn't be hard to get Emma to my car. Meanwhile, the sweet ocean breeze rushed past me as if there had been a vacuum in the room.

"Was she really trying to starve you to death?" I asked incredulously as I walked back to Emma.

"And a little torture when she got bored with that idea." Emma raised one pant-leg to show off some burns, then pointed to her shirt, which was bloodstained.

I swore as the proverbial light dawned. "Was she the one who stabbed you at The Lovage?"

"I really don't know, Alice. I never saw the person who did it, but she had called and asked me to meet her that night so I could get the watch back she had left in the restaurant."

"That ugly—I mean that…"

"I gave her that fake thing." Emma's laugh turned into a cough. "It was ugly, but she wanted it because it looked like a Rolex. Status is a big thing with Jo."

"But she didn't get it back. She tried again last Friday night?"

"You got it. She said I never met her that night I was stabbed! Can you imagine? Anyway, I went down to The Lovage, met her, got it out of the safe, and that's the last thing I remember. I woke up in the car, gagged, with my hands and feet tied. When we got to her apartment, she ungagged me, untied my feet and threatened to kill me if I said or did anything on the way up in the elevator. She had what I thought was a gun in my back. It was the handle of a steak knife. She thought fooling me was very funny."

"Why all this?"

"Years ago, we were lovers. I was just starting out in the restaurant business and met her in a gay bar in San Francisco. Love at first sight for me, at least."

"Your first?"

"Yes." She looked away.

"And nights to remember, so to speak?" I meant my tone to be sympathetic. After all, I did understand.

"Yes." She looked up. "What I didn't know was that she went to straight pickup bars too. That's where she met Peters."

"And she broke it off with you."

"No. She refused to tell me what was going on even when I saw them together at the restaurant opening of a friend. When I asked her, she denied everything. Even when Tony told me about his father's new girlfriend, gave me her name, and told me she was with Peters when Jo had told me she was visiting sick friends, she denied that anything was going on. It was absolutely bizarre. I could see what was happening, and she was telling me it was all my jealous imagination."

"Did you tell Tony about her?"

"I was too ashamed and utterly confused. He never knew."

"But didn't you ever break up? No one can keep something like that going forever."

"I broke it off when I got The Bountiful Harvest going. I just couldn't handle Jo and a new business. But Jo wouldn't let go. I really don't know why, but she sure knew how to ring my bells, and I couldn't shake loose. Just when I thought I might be getting over her, she'd show up and work that old magic. I'd be back in bed with her, all would be fine, and then she'd pull some absurd trick or disappear. I didn't know whether I was coming or going emotionally."

"Is that why…"

"Alice, I could blame Jo if I wanted to for the failure of my restaurant, but I can only blame myself and my own stupidity for falling for the same trick twice. She may have played it, but I was old enough to know better. I did it to myself."

That was more mature than I could be, I thought. Had Frances played those games with me, I'd have been after her like a dog with its tongue hanging out too.

"Can you stand up yet?"

"I think so."

I put my arms around her. "Grab hold and I'll lift."

She swayed for a second but settled on her feet as I held her hands.

"And the favas? Was that her idea too?"

"Yes…"

Suddenly, Emma's eyes widened.

Someone behind me shrieked.

I turned my head.

Jo had a knife in her hand. And she was raising it to strike.

CHAPTER 35

I WAS ON my back, and as totally helpless as a fat, middle-aged turtle. Emma had thrown herself at me, knocked me out of the way of the knife, and grabbed Jo's arm. Above me, the two of them were struggling for the weapon, their feet shuffling on either side of my body.

This was not an equal struggle. Emma was running on adrenaline. That wouldn't last her long. Jo was taller and hadn't been tied up, starved, and left without water in a hot room for far too long. And I didn't have a lot of options. If I bent to one side, I'd knock Emma into Jo, who'd have the strength to push her away and kill both of us before either had the chance to blink. If I bent to the other, I'd knock Jo off balance right into Emma with the same result. With all my weight, I just could not get up fast enough.

Then Jo's foot slid under my neck. It was my only chance to distract her. I grabbed her leg, pulling myself closer, opened my mouth, and brought my teeth down hard on the front of her ankle. I tasted blood.

She screamed, pulling her leg away from my teeth, and kicked me in the ribs, but she stayed upright. I was still floundering on the floor, and Emma was weakening.

"Shit!" I groaned. "We're dead."

Then I heard two of the sweetest words ever spoken: "Freeze! Police!"

Jo kneed Emma in the crotch, and she dropped like a rock

on top of me. The knife clattered to the floor an inch from my nose.

Like a streak, Jo raced away, and, head first, threw herself out the open window.

There was no fire escape there. It was a six-story drop.

CHAPTER 36

AS I CAME into my living room with some hearty, English-style tea and a plate of oatmeal-raisin cookies that Lorenza had whipped up yesterday, I saw Piers sitting on Detective Thompson's black pants. He was purring quite happily, but, knowing him, I was sure he was carefully shedding only his gray hairs on her.

"He's getting fur all over you! Piers, get off her lap. Shoo!" Teapot in hand, I waved ineffectively at him.

The cat moved not one muscle, showed his third eyelid, and continued to purr. He was clearly unimpressed with my show of authority.

"He can sit here. He's a hero."

Indeed, my darling detective did look genuinely relieved about something as she petted the hair-shedding perp.

"Hero?"

"He just saved me."

Did I detect a sheepish look on my Angel's face? I raised my eyebrows questioningly.

"From a spider."

I rounded my mouth in a silent O.

"It was walking straight for me."

I do believe I saw just a bit of red underneath the tan of Detective Thompson's cheeks. I opted for mercy.

"He ate it?"

"He stepped on it. It's…" She waved vaguely toward a corner of the room. "I think it may be over there somewhere."

I went to look. If I had had a magnifying glass, I might have been better able to see the specklike corpse.

"Quite dead," I assured her. "I take it you don't like spiders much?" I asked in some amazement.

She shuddered. "I hate them! They're ugly, creepy, vile things!"

My hero afraid of spiders? I, personally, didn't mind them at all, however. I caught myself before drifting too far into a lovely fantasy of our life together where I could save Angel from the horrors of hostile arachnids and she could...Well, never mind.

"Piers does hunt spiders well," I said with a smile. "Almost as well as you hunt people. I read about your most recent coup with the drug ring."

Thompson's shoulders relaxed now that the menace was confirmed dead and the protective savior was on her lap. But she looked up at me and frowned. "Speaking of catching people, you should have called me, you know, before you went off to find Emma."

"Now I wish I had. Hindsight is great." I looked down at my open hands.

"Don't blame yourself for Jo's death, if that's what you're thinking. Apparently, she was planning to commit suicide after she killed Emma. The officers found three drafted suicide notes."

"But maybe the police would have been able to capture her before she jumped if I had called them first."

"Maybe. And maybe she would have killed Emma anyway and then killed herself as planned. When you're dealing with complex and sometimes conflicting motivations, there aren't always happy endings. At least you weren't killed too."

I bit into a cookie and kept my head down.

Angel smiled. "I must admit I loved that landlord's description of an enormous crazy woman breaking into an apartment. At least you terrorized him enough that he called the police. Alice McDoughall, the Wild Woman of Daly City! Seems he didn't want to admit he let you in until he found out you had probably saved Emma's life. Then he claimed full credit for helping out." She hesitated. "By the way, the officer told me you weren't huge at all."

I wasn't in the mood for being soothed by that or by her softened voice. "And maybe I should have figured out that Didi would call Jo after our little lunch together to warn her."

"I'll grant that. But if you had called the police, they might not have taken you seriously because the story did sound a little crazy. We like to think we can distinguish the nutty stories from the normal but crazy ones, but newspapers are full of reports when we fail. We're only human, and we hate ourselves when we make those mistakes."

"But you would have taken me seriously."

"I would have because I know you. But, if you had called me, maybe I couldn't have convinced the right people in enough time either. We're still a system driven by jurisdictions, paperwork, and, sometimes, egos. You know, country cop and city cop thing."

"But surely someone had suspected Jo in Peters's death?"

"Peters officially died of a heart attack. Fava beans aren't a deadly weapon. Peanuts aren't either, even if you're allergic to them. This was a civil matter between Lorenza and the Peters family. The son finally dropped the lawsuit too. If you hadn't been so dogged about the fava bean business, Alice, the link between Peters, Jo, and Emma might never have been made."

I shrugged my shoulders. "And Emma's disappearance wasn't puzzling?"

"We don't worry about the short absences. Emma had a history of drinking, according to Lorenza. Barring evidence to the contrary, the most probable conclusion would have been that she had gone out on a much-delayed binge. Nor was there anything to link Jo and Emma. Didi knew of some connection, but there was no reason for her to say anything; Jo wasn't in any danger that she could see. Didi would probably have been delighted if Emma had disappeared."

"But surely her disappearance and the stabbing would have…?"

"Jo wasn't a suspect in Emma's stabbing. Without evidence to suggest otherwise, we went with the statistical probability. A botched break-in was the most likely thing to suspect. Emma's statement was hardly enlightening. She remembered zilch." She reached out and patted my hand. "As a police detective who knows the dangers of amateurs getting into dangerous situations with no training or experience, I really shouldn't say this, but you do have good sleuthing ability!"

"Thanks." I smiled at the apprehensive expression on Thompson's face. "But don't worry. I'm not quitting my day job. I don't like violence and death any more than you like spiders."

"That's why I figured I could safely say it." She shuddered. "But no contest. Spiders are worse."

I patted her hand back. It made me feel good to do that.

"I wouldn't care to deal with a body after a six-floor fall either," I said.

"Not a pretty sight. I'll grant you that. Even after all these years, there are some things you never get used to. If you dwell on it, you go nuts."

"Good sleuthing or not, I never did find out how the favas got on the back porch and why." I didn't want to stay on the subject of the uglier parts of police work.

"Jo put them there. She had watched the restaurant and noticed how and when Lorenza and the staff came and went through the back door. She figured someone would think someone else had put the bowl there and forgotten to take it in. And if no one fell for that, maybe she had a backup plan. We don't know."

Of course, I was the one to fall for it. Inwardly, I winced.

"And she found out what the menu was going to be because John always got a heads-up on that before they went. She was good at getting her way, but this time it wasn't hard to persuade Peters to choose the burrito. It was the least unique item. And when Peters wanted to pan a place, he loved to choose something to review that could be lumped in with scads of similar fare. Made the entrée look dull."

Poor Lorenza and stupid me. Jo had been in the driver's seat with both of us just sitting there for the ride. Ride? Ride! Suddenly I thought of one small detail.

"That little red Miata," I said. "That was hers, wasn't it? She was just leaving the night that Lorenza and I got to The Lovage. And I saw it again when I opened the window at Jo's apartment. She was parking behind my car."

"That was hers."

"And maybe at the hospital after Emma was stabbed?" I thought about the woman pulling down her visor in the parking lot as Lorenza pointed out the car to me.

"Possibly. We talked to the head nurse at County. Someone else was at the hospital and asked about her condition just after you left that day. The nurse remembered because she thought it was so nice Emma had so many caring friends. The description generally fit Jo."

"But why all this absurd plotting and planning with the fava beans?"

"According to Emma, Jo wanted to make Peters sick, not kill him. She had this crazy idea that if he got sick and she nursed him back to health, he'd be so grateful he'd marry her. And do you know why she was so panicked? This is a good one. She thought Peters was getting interested in another woman. Guess who?"

"I pass."

"Her sister!"

"But Didi was no threat to her. Peters noticed Jo was acting oddly and thought she was going through something emotional. He thought Didi's company would calm her down."

"And even though she knew about the fava allergy, she didn't know if he was allergic to the cooked or uncooked favas. So she threw them both in."

Thus making them less identifiable to Peters, I thought. "I wonder what was wrong with Jo to begin with?"

"In part, age. Apparently, Jo thought she was getting past her prime, so she was desperate for Peters to marry her. If he didn't, she figured no one would."

"I can't believe any intelligent woman would think that way any more."

"Look around. Not all women are like Lorenza, you, and Emma."

I had never really thought about that.

"How is Emma?" I asked.

"All right. Considering. Jo managed to do a bit more damage to her than Emma told you about. She'll be okay. She's a pretty strong lady."

I felt sick. "I can't believe a woman would ever do something like that to another woman."

"Alice, Jo was a very disturbed young woman. You know, sometimes my husband and I talk about this. Adults like Jo were kids once. Cute little things with a whole exciting future ahead of them. Then something happens, and their world turns twisted and ugly."

I suddenly had a vision of a miniature Peters with a miniature bald spot pounding at his mother with little fists while an equally small Jo, in a little-girl party dress with bows, stands looking on with a tiny knife in her hand. I did not feel especially forgiving.

"How refreshingly liberal of you to think of criminals as innocent little children! I thought all police officers were so sick of the adults that they longed for the good old days when we branded or pilloried lawbreakers and chopped off offending parts. A foot cut off for jaywalking! Both hands for what Jo did to Emma." I crushed what was left of my cookie into a hundred crumbs.

Thompson gave me a tolerant smile and said nothing.

"I didn't mean that. I'm sorry. There are times I am so angered by what people do to others that I forget that justice is not vengeance. If I were on a jury, I'd be so outraged by the murder, I'd want the killer to suffer more than his or her victim. That's one reason I don't believe in the death penalty. It would be so easy to become no better than the killer in my rage for retribution."

"I don't excuse murder, but even I don't like the death penalty. Killing another person is not an easy thing to do, even in war, even in self-defense. With the death penalty, we act as if killing a creature like ourselves is a simple matter of choice, like the person should be able to "just say no" before they pull the trigger. I'm not a bleeding-heart liberal, but I don't think killing the killers is ever going to get us to the 'why' so we can stop it before it happens."

"What do you think are the whys?"

"If I knew that, I could stop crime instead of fighting it."

"But I want people to get what they deserve. Peters may have been a harmless little child, but he grew up to be a snippy little bigot. And Jo? Women aren't supposed to be violent. They aren't supposed to kill. But she almost succeeded with Emma, and maybe she did kill Peters. And she got away with torturing an innocent person. I don't like the fact she took her own life. I want to see society have its justice on her!"

"Maybe the question isn't why Jo tried to kill Emma but why she didn't actually succeed when she had the opportunity? Maybe we need to understand more about why things really happen the way they do before we jump to conclusions."

"Right! Tell Emma in the hospital that she should have compassion for Jo and take comfort that she didn't kill her."

"Actually, Emma did cry for her. She said she was crying because Jo was in such pain that she couldn't help herself, and she was weeping for Didi, who never knew what her sister was really like."

"I still hate Jo. And Peters."

"No law says you have to like them."

"Thanks," I snorted in contempt. "If nothing else, Peters should have lived to be an impotent old man with no one left to pander to him. And Jo should have been made to suffer for what she did and tried to do to Emma."

"With you on the jury, she would have been hanged, drawn, and quartered."

"That isn't funny. I told you I would never serve on a jury with a death penalty. I know I'm being irrational!"

Suddenly, the image of Frances, shattered and bloody, on a cold and impersonal morgue slab flashed into my mind. The image of her murderer laughing on all those beautiful mornings my darling would never enjoy again burned into my brain. Tears welled up and flooded down my cheeks before I could stop them. I was weary of trying to understand the reasons why irrational things happened.

"Damn it, Thompson. I want my simplicities back! Some things just should never happen, that's all!"

Angel Thompson came over and gently held me close to her.

I wept, wept, and wept.

Then the tears weren't just about Frances anymore. They were for Emma, who'd lost something irretrievable when Jo played slash and burn with her heart. I was crying for Lorenza, who'd lost a husband she adored. I wept for Didi, who lost the illusion of a sister. And suddenly I was crying for Jo, because she couldn't make peace with the woman she was when that seemed such a simple thing to me. And I was weeping for myself, a woman who goes through life with her own blinders on and thinking things should just be a certain way. No grays. Thompson was right: Nothing is ever that simple. I hate truth.

"It's okay, Alice. Really, it is. You're exhausted with everything that's been going on since Peters died. For God's sake, give yourself a break. You're not used to this kind of thing."

I shook my head. I didn't want her to talk. I just wanted her to hold me.

"You know, I am very impressed with how you figured everything out. And don't forget that Emma owes her life to you. That isn't something to take lightly."

Thompson's breath tickled my ear. I giggled. So much for hanging on to the tender moment between us. I raised my head and looked at her. She was smiling very gently at me. Her tweed jacket was soaked on the right shoulder from my tears.

"You're humoring me," I said with a final sniff, then picked a few gray cat hairs off her jacket. "By the way, Piers did a superb job of giving your clothes a layer of quality cat hair. I must have a brush somewhere."

"You're changing the subject."

I was, deliberately, before I lost all pride.

"Don't be hard on yourself, Alice. You understand far more than you give yourself credit for. But next time, give me a call first, will you?"

"There won't be a next time," I said with conviction. "Lightning and murder never strike twice in the same place. Livorno has had its excitement for this generation."

"Don't count on it," she replied with a laugh. I think she was teasing me.

"By the way, you called me some time ago, and I never got the chance to find out why." I moved away from her arms with significant regret.

"Oh, I talked to Lorenza about it. I want you two to come over for dinner. I'd like you to meet my husband."

"Thrilled," I sighed.

CHAPTER 37

SO, THE METAPHORICAL dust has finally settled, and life has returned to its expected bucolic little routine. Thank God Livorno has survived its criminal excitement for the century.

And The Lovage is still doing land-office business. In fact, Lorenza is putting in a parking lot. She refused to bulldoze the back of the restaurant. She likes the homey quality that all those flowering, bushy little weeds and horse barn give the place, so the lot is going across the street where a vacant movie theater was torn down. As usual, she's probably right. Right, that is, about everything except the color of the restaurant. I'll never give up on that.

Last night, Doctor and Detective Thompson called. They asked if I'd join them for dinner and an evening of the Emerson String Quartet. I said I would. Of course I like the Emerson, but I have to admit I do so want to see if Thompson will wear a skirt. I still can't believe she's straight, but then my mother wouldn't have either.

They (or more specifically Detective Thompson) also strongly suggested I bring someone with me. Seems they just happened to have a spare ticket. And since they had already invited Lorenza, I knew they meant a date kind of someone.

Why do I see the fine hand of Lorenza in this idea? Probably because now would be the first chance she's had to pair me up after all the distractions following Peters's death. And having Thompson make the suggestion instead of her? Sounds a lot like Lorenza's idea of subtlety to me. (I can just hear her. "She'll listen to you, Angel. She's heard it too long from me.")

Humph.

Of course, my first reaction was to ignore the hint. Then I thought about it. Maybe I should ask Emma, I finally decided. After what she's been through, a pleasant evening with good friends might be just what the doctor ordered, so to speak.

And, as Lorenza would have told me, it really wouldn't kill me to be nice just once, you know.